"You will remain until the villa is completed."

Rafael's fingers sank into her flesh, and Terry slumped, becoming almost acquiescent in his grip. "I may not be your supervisor," he grated, "but I control the work force under my roof, and you won't terminate your duties until I give my permission."

An odd situation had arisen in the starlight beside the *atalaya*. Terry had thought that if she offered Rafael no resistance, he would let her go. Yet his hands continued to grip her shoulders.

Had she wanted to, she could have turned out of his grasp. But some sweet compulsion held her there, and while Terry knew it was dangerous to linger, no part of her could oppose the weakening magnetism of Rafael's nearness.

ROUMELIA LANE
is also the author of these

Harlequin Romances

and this

Harlequin Presents

Lupin Valley

Roumelia Lane

Harlequin Books

TORONTO • NEW YORK • LOS ANGELES • LONDON
AMSTERDAM • PARIS • SYDNEY • HAMBURG
STOCKHOLM • ATHENS • TOKYO • MILAN

Original hardcover edition published in 1982
by Mills & Boon Limited

ISBN 0-373-02536-X

Harlequin Romance first edition March 1983

CHAPTER ONE

To the casual observer in the little fishermen's port of Pollensa, with its blue sweep of bay, windsurfing sails and white pine-fringed beaches, the seasonal changes were subtle indeed. But there were those who recognised the coming of summer in the feathery green sprouting of the beachside tamarisks, lopped ruthlessly to give maximum sunshine to the winter visitor; in the first golden show amid the dark fronds of the date palms fronting the ancient Spanish villas. Pedal boats in neat rows began to appear on the beaches near the town, expensive cruisers bobbed beside previously unattached mooring buoys, and in the bars and cafés with their overflow of chairs and tables across on the beach side of the road the waiters were busy, when not serving drinks, erecting gay fringed awnings.

Terry was not unaware of the heightening atmosphere. The fact that she had been here in this picturesque resort situated at the northernmost tip of the island of Majorca long enough to notice the imperceptibly changing scene filled her with a growing unease. A little dubious this morning about starting out on her usual carefree way, she idled along the garden path of the rented cottage to where a figure sat busy with pen and notepad. 'I've been thinking, I could just as well phone through to Delgado's for these things.' She eyed the shopping list in her hand. 'They always deliver anyway.'

'With your Spanish?' The dark-haired girl looked up from her sun chair expressively. She was not pretty, but she had good features, if a little sharp, and a

5

groomed air. 'And anyway,' she added most of her attention still with the figures on the notepad, 'you know you enjoy the walk to town.'

'I love it,' Terry sighed. 'The scenery round here is out of this world ⟩ . . but it doesn't seem right spending all morning doing a simple shopping chore.'

'Why not? Why the gloom all at once, poppet?' The question was put discerningly, but not at the expense of more rapid calculations being made on the notepad.

Terry decided it was time to speak up. 'The truth of it is, Verna,' she said, straightening her slim frame, 'we've been here for days now and we haven't done anything about this job we're supposed to have come out here to tackle.'

Her colleague lifted her head and placed the pen down on the notepad placatingly, an action which did little to dispel the calculating look that remained in her eyes. 'I've told you to leave that side of the business to me,' she smiled. 'There's a lot you don't understand about the work we're in, Terry. Things like letting down the image. You don't go rushing out to set up shop the moment you've arrived on an assignment. For one thing, this could indicate that you need the money, and if we're to hold our own with the crop of first-class interior decorators there are in this part of the world that's the last impression we want to give. Don't you see?' Her manner became more intense. 'This is the chance of a lifetime, the biggest thing we've swung yet. Trust me to handle it my way. The Marqués will approach us in his own good time. It's understood that when you reach our status in the profession it isn't done to make the first move.'

'I suppose you're right,' Terry agreed reluctantly.

'I am. Now don't you worry your head about these things.' Verna gave her an encouraging pat. 'Off you go and enjoy yourself, and leave it to me to do what's best for the business.'

'All right ... if you're sure there's nothing I can do ...' Needing little persuasion to be on her way, Terry drifted along the path towards the gate. She waved before turning out into the avenue. Verna would see to everything. Verna always knew what was best.

As she crossed the road towards the sea the light of expectancy returned to Terry's eyes at the thought of the morning that lay before her. Life for her in this tiny resort with its backcloth of craggy mountains had blossomed into various stages of contentment. She loved pottering in the cottage garden with its semi-tropical foliage, and devising a meal in the spotless kitchen. But more than this, the prospect of a walk where the white beaches made little coves on the way to town filled her with girlish pleasure.

She didn't feel much of a professional sauntering along in her lilac cotton dress which had seen many washings. Her light brown hair she wore parted down the middle and two deep waves winged casually away from fair eyebrows, leaving the rest to bounce as it liked just above her shoulders. She didn't have Verna's sophisticated manner or her clever sense of dress. But then Verna was the brains behind their partnership.

Over the road a wide avenue was lined with smart apartment blocks whose open-plan gardens showed green lawns and bordering roses. At the end flower-decked balconies framed the view of the sparkling sea and the yellow and blue hulls of diminutive sailing craft moored in the shallows.

As Terry turned the corner she was met by the familiar scents of beach pines and warm sand and the scene that never failed to stir her; that of the bay, circular and apparently without outlet, and across it, seemingly miles away but no more than a leisurely half

hour's walk from here, the white houses and
commercial buildings of the port of Pollensa.

Just a little way along she came to the Hotel Esperanza.
To Terry's mind it must be about the loveliest hotel on
the island. The only one along this stretch of coastline, it
had an air of exclusivity that did nothing to detract from
the charm of its design. Its two-tiered white balustraded
terraces fronting guest rooms were reminiscent of a
bygone era, and across the path where giant pines and
tamarisks leaned seawards the sun-terrace retained an
air of the early Twenties with its basketwork loungers
and white metalwork tables for drinks.

The guests were very elegant. Terry had seen them
in the evening, the women in their rose-pink and
lavender gowns, the men in roll-collared dinner jack-
ets. Sun-bronzed and rosy after a day spent in and out
of the sea, they would chat in the flattering light of
dusk on the terrace creating a sense of well-being and
the feeling that there were no struggles in the world.

Starting from the centre of the sun terrace a pebble-
dash jetty had been built for the mooring of the patrons
sailing craft, though anyone could use it. That was one
nice thing that Terry was discovering about Spanish
hotels. Nobody minded if you were a resident or not.
You could sit at any table and order a drink, even swim
in the pool if there was one. And certainly nobody
would glance at you twice if you felt like wandering
round some plush interior. The same easy-going
atmosphere prevailed at the Hotel Esperanza, and
guests watched with a benign air the activities of visitors on the public beach, glad of any diversion from
their constant turning, as though on a spit, under the
browning sun.

This morning quite a few chairs were occupied on
the sun terrace, but Terry had become used to picking
her way through on to the jetty. She had some bread

in a paper bag in her hand. Feeding the fish might not be a very elegant pastime, but it was one she enjoyed.

The water was so clear one could see the tiny hermit crabs, no bigger than a thumbnail, scurrying along the sandy bottom. The shoals of fish which explored the scaly sides of the jetty varied in size from the minute specimens looking like a shower of orange and green sparks as the sun caught their bodies, to the great big prowlers, over a foot long, always on the lookout for titbits.

Feeding these hotel pets was a fascinating occupation. From the first ball of bread dropped over the side parents and offspring would converge in a wild threshing and twisting in the water, showing glistening pink undersides, each nudging the bread with mouths that made short work of the offering.

Terry was so absorbed in giving them plenty of exercise with the supply from her bag that she didn't notice the laughing group making their way along the jetty; not until her place at the edge began to feel a little precarious. A dozen people drifting by and not paying particular attention to where they were going didn't leave an awful lot of space on a width less than a couple of yards wide.

She forgot the fish for the moment, not that there were many about after the noisy passage, and watched the activity near a tethered power-boat. It was a gleaming piece of equipment, coffee-cream in colour, with rich dark brown leather seats of which there were ample to accommodate the animated group. The obvious owner, a man in faultless pale slacks and shirt, turned a suave white smile their way. One could imagine him zipping expertly over the waves without getting so much as a spot of spray on his impeccable attire. He was an impressive personality with well-defined olive-skinned features and shining black hair inclined to be wavy. But his air of distinction, as far as Terry was concerned, did not excuse him cluttering up the jetty with his friends.

They were a smart, sophisticated crowd. Two or three of them looked as if they were Spanish, the rest were a mixture of English and French. Clearly their host was a man of the world. The soigné women in their heavy-rimmed sunglasses and expensive beach clothes were undoubtedly aware of his lady-killing techniques.

While they were finding their places in the power-boat assisted by the men in the party the revving up of the outboard motor added to the commotion. Terry despaired of coaxing any fish after that, and true enough, when the dashing sea-craft had finally taken off, the suave individual at the wheel, even the hermit crabs had dived under the sand.

She watched its turbulent departure in disgust. Hotel people, obviously. Well, it was to be hoped their holiday was in its last stages. The way they had taken over the jetty, anyone would think they owned it personally! Though she thought in the plural her gaze remained fixed on the commanding figure at the wheel of the power-boat, then, more than glad to forget the incident, she turned away. The whole of the walk to town lay before her and she was soon lost in the beauty of these new surroundings.

The path, shaded by trees, meandered this way and that. At one side the translucent waters of the bay washed up on minute stretches of sand broken up by private landing stages for boats, and stone-built platforms holding lounging chairs. These belonged to the villas at the other side of the path. Most of the beach-side mansions had been modernised and were let now to summer holidaymakers, but there were still a few that retained a faded air of magnificence. Through the day they were shuttered up in true Spanish style, but if one was to walk this way in the evening it was possible to catch glimpses of mellow-lit interiors with stout dark furniture and oil paintings on the walls of faces and scenes long since gone.

Once Terry had spied a prim little Spanish maid behind neatly clipped privet bushes, laying supper on a long heavy wooden table beside a window open to the warm night. In the interior, beyond the room with its faded tapestries, the loud voices of the family sounded to be legion in numbers. Though none would venture out in the daytime when the arch-enemy the sun ruled, a few drifted out to sit for a chat in their chairs overlooking the gentle lap of the waves in the cool starlight, and the elderly especially could be heard re-living among themselves, one fancied, the leisurely days of the past.

Terry knew every facet of the walk by now; the way some of the giant pines had leaned over the years, leaving only sufficient headroom along the path, to breathe the cool air of the sea. One or two directly along the walker's route had had to be sawn off at ground level to make way for happily padding tourist feet. But while one lamented this there was some compensation in noticing that other veterans had been given a helping hand, for here and there sagging boughs and lurching trunks were supported by brick-built columns provided by the thoughtful council authorities. One old tamarisk had not survived some long-ago gale, but though half of its roots were bare in the sand below the path, a mop of feathery green valiantly gazed at its reflection inches above the crystal water.

Terry drifted at a leisurely pace and once she had passed the more spacious beaches fronting the town she made for the central marina. Here one could see the fishing boats and the men scaling and cleaning their catch, and read the fascinating names on the hulls of all manner of sailing craft.

It was well past noon when she turned reluctantly at last to the shops and headed for Delgado's. Here they catered mainly to the vast number of foreign residents in the area as well as tourists renting villas, and the three floors, though each little larger than an average living room, were an Ali Baba's cave to someone stranded in a land of strange-tasting Spanish food. There were cheeses from France, German sausage and rye-bread, all kinds of Scandinavian luxuries, from caviar to tinned smoked herring, Austrian sweetmeats, English tea and heaven knew what else on the glittering shelves.

Of course Terry's list didn't include anything but the basic essentials for a meal. She didn't feel easy about squandering money on exotic products. Verna was always encouraging her to feel free to indulge in any fancy she cared for, for the table, but Terry supposed she could never quite shake off the feeling that there was something precarious about the way they made a living.

She had crossed most of the things off her list when there was a commotion out on the roadside. From her position at the back of the shop, the curving staircase to the other floors between her and the doorway, she saw a lively group alighting from a sporty-looking automobile. Her lips tightened when she recognised them as belonging to the set who had commandeered the jetty earlier that morning. So they had grown tired of sightseeing round the bay in a gleaming sea-chariot, and now their urbane host was at the wheel of an equally resplendent road machine. One look at the dark-haired figure told her that she hadn't been mistaken in her rapid identification of his friends. There couldn't be more than one man with his aristocratic charm on the island.

Luckily she was nearly through with her shopping and as there were only four or five of them in the group this time she wasn't likely to see much of them in the almost deserted interior. She went to the cold meat section and bought fresh slices of ham, and splashed on a bag of imported mushrooms rather than risk the floppy pancake-like local ones. There was nothing resembling fresh corn-on-the-cob, so it would have to be a tin of sweet corn. Unfortunately these were on the first floor, but as it was one of the last items she would have to collect for her basket, which was becoming a weight to carry around, the sooner she got it finished with the better.

Alfredo, like shopkeepers the world over, had a penchant for stacking tinned foods in high unwieldy pyramids. As the tins of sweet corn were large ones Terry had her work cut out selecting one which wouldn't dismantle the whole display. She was fingering a tin tentatively when the hotel group came gusting up, attracted among other things, it seemed, by the shelves of wines and liquors lining the nearby wall. Of course their main objective would be drink, Terry thought sourly.

She had chosen a stable tin of sweet corn when two or three sets of arms reached round her for bottles of sherry. For a moment she was left with about as much space as she had had on the jetty, but this time something had to give. Pressured to shift her position, she heard the ominous rattle of the sweet corn tins and to her horror saw on the other side of the swaying metal pile an old Majorcan woman in black shawl peering on a lower shelf at the cheaper local wines.

'*Cuidado, señora!*' She rushed round and pushed the old woman clear just as a heavy tin bounced near her

ankles, followed by another brushing her shin. She
tensed under the barrage, knowing there was no escape
for herself, but curiously nothing else happened.

After the first half dozen tins had crashed heavily to
the floor a pair of hands with a firm look about them
steadied the pyramid, rapidly resettling the foundation
and rearranging weaker sections of the construction. It
was all done within seconds, after which the driver of
the smart car and the racy power-boat raised the
startled old woman from her cowering position and
addressed her in the local tongue.

Her faded mahogany eyes almost popped out of her
head while he spoke with her. Hurriedly she made it
known that she had come to no harm and with a flicker
of gratitude crossing her wrinkled features at his concern she turned and shuffled off, the cheap table wine
apparently forgotten in her haste to make herself
scarce.

Terry supposed it must be old people who yielded
equably to dominating ways. Her own slim shoulders
squared as she reached for what she had originally
come for and had a tin of sweet corn placed in her
hand. 'That was a foolhardy gesture, *señorita*.
Commendable but unecessary. I had noted the *abuela*
and would have acted myself to avert disaster.'

Barely giving her attention to the man who spoke to
her in alien English, Terry replied, 'Your best bet
would be to confine your parties to more spacious surroundings, *señor*. Or do you always monopolise public
places when you're on holiday?'

There was a silence and then, 'Dropping your titbits
of bread to the fish on the Hotel Esperanza jetty is a
charming pastime, *señorita*, but you must accept that it
can also be a vulnerable one.'

After that Terry sought to end the conversation
abruptly. 'As no harm has been done,' she eyed the

littered tins, 'I think we can consider the matter closed. Excuse me, *señor*.'

'One moment!' She sensed that the dark eyes were blazing. 'You have had an unpleasant shock. You will allow me to accompany you downstairs.'

'That will not be necessary. I'm quite all right.' She retrieved her shopping basket and added, 'If I were you I should get back to your sporty limousine. This is a holiday town and you never know, you may be breaking the parking laws taking up all that space.'

Again there was a steely pause, but he himself was not idle, for one of those competent hands had joined hers on the handle of her wire basket. 'I insist on seeing you safely to the floor below.' His voice was menacingly curt.

Terry eyed the strong hand beside hers, then raised a pointed blue glance to the detestably arrogant face. 'Good day, *señor*,' she said evenly.

For a moment she felt that he was too close for comfort. His thin aristocratic nostrils dilated, and the hand beside hers on the basket showed no sign of relenting.

It was a footstep on the stair which broke the suspicion of a deadlock. Seeing that chaos had been avoided, the rest of the hotel group had disappeared, but Alfredo must have heard the commotion, for he came hurrying up the steps, a well-built man with something of a paunch which left him a little out of breath.

Like the old lady his eyes protruded somewhat when he saw the erect figure a short distance from Terry now, on the upper floor. He began to scrabble for the tins, but a few words of clipped Spanish brought him to his feet. A brief conversation took place, during which Alfredo nodded frequently. Terry had started towards the stairs when the storekeeper gripped her basket with his large fist and said with an embarrassed smile, '*Permiteme, señorita.*'

'Thank you, Alfredo.' Terry was not sorry to let the weight go this time. She and the Majorcan trader had become friends of a sort. He knew a few words of English and she had picked up the odd one here and there in Spanish, and between them they always managed a joke or two when she visited his store.

At the till on the ground floor she told him, 'Would you put these on our account as usual, Alfredo, and deliver them when you can.'

Out of doors her cheeks felt a little warm in the sunshine. She noted the sleek sports machine briefly before crossing the road back to the sea side of the town.

CHAPTER TWO

THE white sand was powdery and cool underfoot. Terry took off her sandals and trailed her feet in the tepid overspill of waves. By the time she had covered half the distance of the return journey round the bay the incident in the food store had slipped from her mind.

As she strolled in the shade the view framed here and there by the huge curving bole of a pine and its greenery was of the blue-blue sea with sometimes the colourful sails of a gliding yacht or a white tripper vessel chugging over the waves, to complete the picture; and always the green-tufted rocks of the Amora mountains across where the ancient city of Alcudia lay; peaks whose looming proximity in the haze lent a mystic quality to the bay and all that took place there.

Wholly appreciative of her surroundings, Terry reminded herself that it was Verna's expertise that had brought them to this paradisical corner of the world. As long as she had known Verna she had never seen her at a loss when it came to furthering their career. From the very first moment the two of them had met Terry had found herself in Verna's capable hands, despite her shy reluctance at the outset.

It had all started that rainy afternoon when Verna had come to see the flat in Earl's Court. Terry's roommate had left at almost a minute's notice to get married and, anxious to find someone to take over half the expenses of the rather rambling first floor, she had put an advert in the evening paper.

Verna liked the flat. She not only liked it, she was

fascinated and intrigued by it. She gazed at the roomy kitchen with its neat white fitments and asked, 'Whose idea was it to put beige vinyl wallpaper with lemon-coloured woodwork?'

'Mine, I suppose,' Terry had shrugged. 'The windows were a bit gaunt in here, but there's not much light with the building opposite. I thought a little bit of light gloss would soften them, and the hand-crocheted net hung straight at three-quarter height helped.' Conversationally she had added, 'I had the same trouble in the second bedroom, but it was easier there to disguise the eyesore with pretty curtains.'

Verna retraced her steps along the corridor to take in again the deep turquoise walls and white lampshades and coverlets. 'You mean you did this too!'

Terry had laughed apologetically then. 'I'm guilty of titivating in most rooms, I'm afraid. It's a hobby of mine.'

'A hobby? Then what do you do for a living, for heaven's sake?'

'Saleslady,' Terry had grimaced. 'I work in the wallpaper and carpeting section at Bailfords.'

'The big store on Potter Street with umpteen floors given over to house furnishing requisites?'

'That's the one. Being able to buy just the right colour cushion from my wages and experimenting with curtain samples started me off, I suppose. But anyone with my job could have done what I've done here.'

'You underestimate your ability, Terry.' The grey eyes viewing the rest of the interior were shrewd. 'It takes more than having all the things on hand to create a pleasing balance; colour sense, for instance, the ability to know what blends in a room, an eye for matching detail—and I'd say you've got the lot.'

Verna was vague about her own working life. It appeared that she hadn't got a job at the moment, and those she had had, had fallen far short apparently of what she was looking for. But she paid a month's rent in advance, and as payment was due the following day Terry had no complaints with that.

Her efforts to soften the Victorian gloom of the flat with a little life and colour continued to be a source of speculative interest to the other girl, and one evening during the second week of her stay when Terry had come home exhausted after a day on her feet Verna had said, 'You're a fool to wear yourself out working for a liveable wage. With your talents you could rake in ten times as much as an interior designer.'

Terry had smiled wanly. 'That's a swish title for someone who slaps a bit of paint around and throws in a few oddments to match.'

'Self-glory is not one of your strong points, is it?' Verna observed without humour. 'Maybe you don't know it, but people are going mad for someone with your gifts these days. Everybody's on to this indoor transformation thing and there just aren't enough interior decorators to go round.'

Terry's thoughts were more with supper which still had to be prepared. She replied, rising, 'I'll admit I've enjoyed touching up here, but I wouldn't want to do it for other people. For one thing, I wouldn't know where to start.'

'I know quite a few names in town. I bet I could get you launched.'

The suggestion was made steadily. Terry might have a reserved nature, but she had smiled astutely then. 'If you did I'm afraid I'd be an awful flop. I couldn't go to parties and flannel around people for work. I'm not the arty type.'

'Neither am I, but I could work at it,' Verna had replied thoughtfully.

Terry wasn't completely blind to her abilities.

Dalveen, the girl who had left to get married, was
always telling her she ought to do something about her
decorating skills. But she knew herself best, and the
thought of working in a job which would entail mixing
with sophisticated professionals filled her with a kind
of panic.

That was why she was riveted three evenings later
when Verna met her in the hall of the flat to announce,
'We're in business! Charles and Debra Hollingwood—
you know, of the Hollingwood jewellers—are off to
America for a two-month stay. They've bought an
apartment in Knightsbridge so that they can have a
base in London when they return and we've got the
job of giving it a face-lift while they're away!'

Terry had dropped down in the first available chair.
'But where? . . . How? . . .'

'I know—I don't waste time once an idea appeals,'
Verna had pulled a face happily. 'Actually the
Hollingwoods are friends of a friend of a friend of
mine. I invited them here this afternoon. They loved
everything about the flat and have given us carte
blanche with their place in Knightsbridge.'

'But you don't understand!' Terry's face was white.
'The idea's horrendous! I may be only a working girl,
but I do happen to know that professional interior
decorators are pretty worldly types; something I'm not.
Just the idea of meeting people like the Hollingwoods
makes me want to run a mile!'

'You don't have to meet anyone if you don't want
to,' Verna said in a slow deliberate way.

'But that's crazy! You may have got a free hand with
the Hollingwoods, but others will want to talk about
colour schemes and room plans, and think of the social
parley that will have to be lived through to get just a
smattering of what's required. No, thanks,' Terry
smiled grimly. 'I haven't got the make-up for that kind

of thing. I'd be no good as a trendy vendor of house styles.'

'All right, you've made your point,' Verna's tones were soothing, 'but it needn't make any difference. Listen. When the Hollingwoods came and looked round here this afternoon, I told them . . .' she hesitated slightly, '. . . I gave them to understand that the ideas on colour and layout were my own. They think I dreamed it all up.'

Terry blinked. But before she could mouth her confusion Verna went on, 'You don't like the limelight, all right? I don't mind it. I've got no talent for interior decorating, but I've proved I can play the part *and* get the work. What difference does it make if you do the job and I take the credit? We'll both be working at what we're cut out for and sharing the profits.'

'But wouldn't that be dishonest?' Terry asked, still in a mist.

'I don't see how. We'll be selling a much needed service, not our individual personalities, and as long as we give satisfaction who's to worry?'

'Nevertheless it is misleading.' Terry didn't feel right about any of it. 'And how are you going to cope when you've got to give advice on the general arrangements of an interior?'

'I've already thought it all out.' Unworried, Verna tapped her chin practically with a forefinger. 'What we've got to do now is get to work on the Hollingwoods' apartment. They'll be away two months, and in that time we've got to show them, and other potential customers, that we can compete with the better known interior decorators in town.'

'Two months!' Terry let out a wail and eyed the other girl pityingly. 'You haven't asked me how long it's taken me to make the improvements here. Do you realise I've been working on the flat, on and off, for four years!'

'But I know something you don't know.' Verna only smiled. 'There are workmen to do one's bidding when one turns professional. We won't be expected to paint and varnish and stick on our own choice in wallpaper, we'll have skivvies for that. As for the furniture and expensive bric-à-brac, you can let me know your ideas and leave the buying to me.'

Somehow Terry went through with it. Perhaps her qualms were eased by the fact that her daily routine changed hardly at all. Bailfords was one of the most exclusive stores in town and as a saleslady there she was able to wander through the household treasures of the five floors in her spare time. She actually enjoyed visualising one room and then another of the Knightsbridge apartment. She had visited it the first weekend to make a mental note of the interior, and Verna with typical foresight had had a long talk with a local bank manager and obtained a loan to cover the cost of fitting it out.

To Terry it became just another hobby. She dreamed up ingenious ways of hanging curtains while she lay in bed at night and envisaged what she could put in that last bare corner of the Knightsbridge living room. Then one evening Verna came home after a re-union with the Hollingwoods to say that they were highly delighted with their new home, and she waved a cheque in her hand to prove it.

From then on there had been no turning back. Verna—she had been Vera Walthall in those days—had at last found something on which to unleash her ambitions. It was as though she had been keyed up all her adult life, poised for the opportunity that had not yet offered itself. It had only needed one meeting with Terry to set all her pent-up drive into motion.

tion, 'His title is the Marqués del Alcázar. The family seat, as they say, is in Madrid, but there are apparently age-old connections with the island of Majorca. He's the local grandee, so I'm told, in a small, close-knit community, tourists excepted, north of the island. He's just had a brand new villa built there. The Langfords introduced me to him. He liked their interiors and—well, to cut a long story short, he's engaged me officially to work on the property.'

'Congratulations.' Terry breathed a little easier. It could have been worse. But a Spanish villa! One day Verna would reach too high, then they would both come tumbling down.

As the realisation percolated through she said, quietly aghast, 'Verna, there's a big difference between the Langfords' modest mews house and some Spanish nobleman's domain. I don't know the first thing about Spanish decor. I haven't even been to Spain!'

'No worries,' Verna waved a hand blithely. 'The Marqués wants it designed with an international flavour. You can work as you've been doing up to now. That's always been our theme, anyway.'

Terry recognised that rigorous determination in her colleague to see a thing through and sighed, 'All right. Let me have the dimensions when you can and extensive photographic detail. It's only a couple of hours in a plane, I believe. Little more than popping over to Paris——'

'Er . . .' Verna stopped her with a hesitant gesture, 'when I said you can work as you've been doing up to now, I didn't mean that we're to be given a free hand like we get over here. The Spaniards don't operate like that. Their own work force is perhaps a little indolent and they've grown accustomed to being on hand to keep an eye on results. This job is going to involve a stay on the island.'

'Well, have a good trip,' Terry shrugged philosophically. 'There's always the phone, I suppose.'

'You're not with me, pet.' Verna's self-possessed smile drooped slightly. '*I* can't go to Majorca on my own. On the face of it I may *be* the interior decorator, and I may be able to spin a yarn to the Marqués, but it's you who does all the clever things with furniture and hangings. You'll have to come too, to feed me the backing I need.'

'Me?' Terry paled. While Verna was playing the figurehead screening her from the business side which she disliked, she had never felt greatly involved. But now their routine of letting Verna take all the bows out front while she dabbed happily in the background wasn't going to work. She had never thought it would. And the thing she had dreaded most was here. She was going to have to take an active part in the deceit.

Clutching at straws, she asked, 'How will you explain my presence to the Marqués?'

'Simple. I'll say you're my assistant. I've already discussed it with the Marqués anyway and he's arranging accommodation for two, so the sooner we get packed the better.'

As usual Verna had it all worked out.

A shaft of sunlight pierced through the fronds of a palm and Terry smiled gently to herself as she walked. She mustn't be too hard on her colleague. Verna was a wizard at business and knew all about life at twenty-seven, and Terry, five years her senior, was still learning from her.

When she got back to the cottage Verna was still in the garden. Her pocket calculator and notepad were on the table beside her, but she was now reclining in a black two-piece swimsuit, her thinnish body and limbs well oiled and already beginning to acquire an attractive tan.

After a leisurely shower Terry made a cold lunch and later washed the dishes while Verna prepared for an afternoon in town.

Not one to waste an opportunity, the other girl had been using the time by making herself known as an interior designer among the rich foreign residents around Pollensa, and was now friendly with people on a par with the Hollingwoods and Langfords who had come to live abroad. But unlike their social counterparts in England the island set didn't gather in stately country homes or smart city restaurants. Instead, in worn shorts and tee-shirts and yachting plimsolls, they grouped under the gay awnings of the café forecourts, or over on the marina near the fishing boats. The sunshine has a way of levelling all strata of society. They didn't even mind using the Coach House pub as their general headquarters, although it was not a pub in the English sense of the word, being long and low and windowless, and strung with hams and garlic and day and night lighting and the heavy sweet redolence of olive oil. It was here where Verna spent most of her time.

She came through into the kitchen now, in strawberry pink slacks and blouse. 'I don't expect I'll be back until late,' she said, fastening an expensive gold coin pendant under the collar of her blouse. 'And don't feel guilty about putting your feet up for a while. From what I've heard it's typical of the Marqués to allow us ample time to settle in.'

'Is he well known around the town?' Terry asked out of idle interest.

'Among the locals he's God,' Verna said with a laugh. 'His family name, so I hear, goes back to the days of the African Corsairs in the thirteenth century and their eventual routing from the town by a swashbuckling descendant. And to ordinary fisherfolk, especially the venerating Majorcans, that's grounds for considerable respect. As for the foreign element,' she smoothed her hair with a look of professional complacency, 'the Marqués is someone they would all like to say they know, but few possess his calling card.'

'He sounds as if he believes his own publicity,' Terry joked, hanging up the tea towel. 'I bet he's lofty, condescending and a bore.'

'If he is it doesn't show,' Verna smiled reflectively. 'I've only met him once, but what I saw was a man with Latin charm and manners that had the ladies in a tiz.'

'What was he doing at the Langfords' party?'

'Slumming, I expect.' Verna's caustic humour didn't spare past patrons. 'Half the Spanish nobility have friends in London. I suppose he was one of a party invited to admire the mews house . . . and lucky for us that he was.'

Terry sighed. 'I wish I had your practical approach,' she said heavily. 'Coming out here on a commission might be all right, but I can't help feeling that in one way we're a pair of cheats.'

'I sell the product and you provide the merchandise. Have we ever had any complaints?' The other girl was gaily incredulous that there should be any discomfort, and watching her Terry remarked, 'You're a glutton for work, Verna, but I've never seen you this enthusiastic before.'

'As I've explained to you before, chick,' Verna pointed a manicured finger her way, 'we stand to make a sizeable sum of money for our services. And besides,' there was something secretive about her smile, 'we've never had quite so interesting a set-up as this before.'

A few minutes later she was taking the hired car

down the drive, and waving her off, Terry sensed that for all that one meeting Verna had been greatly impressed by what she had seen of the Marqués del Alcázar.

CHAPTER THREE

THE cottage was one of several newish constructions in a holiday urbanisation laid out at the foot of a jagged granite and green peak. Shady plane trees lined the avenues and some of the houses were of villa proportions with expensive cars jutting out from open garages and tall eucalyptus trees rustling on smooth lawns. But tucked away on its own in a cul-de-sac, with just two bedrooms, living room, kitchen and bathroom, their habitation was, to Terry at least, a cottage.

It had a roof of rippling red tiles, white walls and little jutting terraces and balconies which gave it a Mediterranean flavour. Alongside the garden wall swept the undulating foothills of the granite peaks, and there was a wildness here and a feeling of remoteness that contrasted strangely with the comfortable amenities the little white house offered.

The garden was heaven after knowing only flat life. Terry had grown up in her parents' garden home in a Sussex village, but there had been little time for visiting during her working years in London. Here there were the scarlet, salmon pink and peach-coloured trumpets of the hibiscus; budding oleanders, carpets of fig marigold, climbing wax-plant, fragrant and creamy white with red centres, and all the semi-tropical greenery which seemed to abound in the island gardens, like the spiky palm known as Spanish Dagger, the lacy hangings of the pepper tree, and majestic Mexican cactus. It was a small garden but cleverly designed to give a feeling of space.

Terry had been toying with the idea of putting a few

pots around. She hated being idle and it would be fun
to see what she could actually produce herself from
cuttings gathered on her walks. It would soon be dusk
and there was no sign yet of Alfredo's delivery van
with the groceries she had purchased that morning.
She smiled to herself as she sorted out trowel and
watering can for her work. She had heard that no one
ever hurried in Spain; and in Majorca, she was discovering, the locals were even more regardless of time.
Anyhow, she and Verna had grown into the habit of
dining late like everyone else. This was one way of
adapting to the tardy ways of the islanders.

Plastic pots were hardly examples of typical local
craftsmanship, she thought wryly, but they were all
she had been able to find on a previous shopping trip,
and in the semi-shade at the side of the house only she
would know they were there. In a blue glazed-cotton
dress which could be easily rinsed through should it
become grubby with soil she knelt at her task, glad to
have something to do.

She had potted all but one of her cuttings and the
first stars were beginning to show through the electric
blue sky of evening when Alfredo's van finally
appeared. She had heard it chugging along the avenues,
for like all the tradesmen's vehicles in these parts it
was decrepit and always seemed about to gasp its last
breath. Alfredo didn't always deliver himself.
Sometimes he sent one of the youths who helped him
in the supermarket, which was why Terry paid no particular attention when a slimmer form than that of the
gross storekeeper proceeded up the drive. But then
something about the carriage of the figure transporting
the carton of groceries, the pale slacks, even in the
gloom too tailored for a delivery boy, brought her to
her feet. Either her eyes were playing tricks on her
or——

'Where would you like me to deposit your order, *señorita*?' That alien English again. And yes, it *was* the holidaymaker who thought he owned the hotel jetty and half the port of Pollensa as well! But what was he doing here?

Coldly she indicated the lighted kitchen doorway. 'You can put them on the table inside. And if your latest act of playing errand boy is meant to be amusing, *señor*, I'm afraid I find it too late in the day for jokes.'

'You continue to make it difficult for me to apologise, yet all the English are not so straitlaced, I know.' His smile was pained and teasing after he had done as she had requested.

'It was hardly necessary to go to the lengths of taking over Alfredo's steam-engine of a van to bring up something I'd quite forgotten.' Having said this Terry paused to look inside herself and was surprised to find that it was not entirely the truth. She might have erased her brush with this man from her mind, but it had not faded from her consciousness. And the mild disturbance she had been feeling all day could have explained her attacking the pots for the sake of something to do.

'I persuaded Alfredo to trust me with his grocery contraption so that I could enquire after you personally.' Her caller looked faintly grim. 'You acted recklessly this morning, shielding an old woman with your own insubstantial frame. The weight of one tin could have crushed a foot or snapped an arm. I knew that some of the tins brushed you and the thought has unsettled me all day.'

'You could have saved yourself the trip, *señor*.' Terry's voice remained level. 'As you can see, I am still in one piece.'

'*Cielo!* But it is a little aloof and unforgiving, that piece.' The figure in the shadows altered his stance. 'I will apologise for my friends if you too will say you are sorry.'

'Me? What do I have to apologise for?'

'For your lack of understanding in an incident that could have been smoothed over on the spot.'

'Smoothing over the result of bad manners, you mean?'

'I'll admit my friends are a little exuberant, but this is a holiday island, *señorita*.'

'For some.' Terry pointedly packed the soil round the cutting in the last pot.

'So! You are one of these who must always think of work. You have some career, perhaps, which blinds you to the pleasures of life, to the enjoyment of everyday things. You are content to ignore the occasional romance of one's surroundings and even that of the heart.'

'I . . . didn't say that, *señor*.'

'Then the young man who will one day come between you and that which makes you so serious will also require that zero temperature of English blood in his veins.' The faintly mocking tones prompted Terry to reply, 'At least you need suffer no such inhibitions, *señor*. The ladies in your party are beautiful and obviously appreciative of your charms.'

'But alas they are the wives of my friends, and for this reason I must be on my best behaviour. Lovely ladies are twice the temptation when they are out of reach.'

'With your experience, *señor*, I hardly need convincing of that.'

Terry saw the glisten of his autocratic smile in the star-glow. 'You disdain experience, *señorita*, but that is just your youth. A woman of maturity would feel otherwise. After all, how is a man to lead the way if he knows nothing of love?'

'I'm sure your lady friends recognise this asset in you, *señor*.'

There was an amused pause and then, 'And you . . . you are not even curious about a man of the world such as I?'

'I'd rather put up with my youth, *señor*. It makes for a more stable existence, which is what I'm used to.'

'Ah yes, the career.'

That was the second time he had referred to her work. If he only knew, she thought wryly, how she hated certain facets of her job!

His outline was silhouetted against the light of the doorway. His face in the shadows appeared to be darkly enigmatic. Lips curving, black hair shining, he bowed stiffly from the waist and said formally, 'Permit me to introduce myself. I am Rafael de Quiso.'

There was a silence and breaking it, he remarked, 'You do not wish to share such confidences, *verdad*? but I know a little about you.'

'From Alfredo, of course.'

He made the considered reply, 'Your name may be on the grocery bill, but I would wish to hear it from your lips, not that of your provision merchant.'

He waited, and something about his manner forced her to respond 'I'm . . . Terry Heatherton.'

'Yes, it has an English ring, that Heatherton,' he mused aloud, 'of cool open spaces, I think. But *Terree* for a girl I have never heard. It is a man's name in your country, is it not?'

'In my case it's short for Teresa,' she explained.

'Ah! Teresa.' He pronounced it Tayraysa. 'But yes, it is *el título* of one of our most revered saints.'

Fleetingly Terry wondered what part of Spain he came from. Madrid perhaps, or Cordoba. Or was it Seville? She could imagine him riding on a proud black stallion in sombrero and dark suit, a Spanish beauty in brilliant frilled dress before him in the saddle at the Seville fair. He had the hauteur for that.

He was frowning with distaste, she noticed, and coming out of her reverie she heard him say, 'What is this penchant for corruption in names? In Spain we prefer to keep the beauty of expression, especially in a birthname such as yours.'

'Another of our weird English customs,' Terry replied. She had finished her work with the pots and pointedly brushing off her hands she added, 'And now, if you will excuse me, *señor*, I must go indoors.'

'But I am still waiting!' There was something both imperious and teasing in his manner. 'I have made my apology, no?'

Aware of what he was hinting, Terry shrugged. 'Very well. I'm sorry for not being more understanding in the supermarket. How's that?'

His hard white smile showed momentarily in the shadows. 'I would have preferred a little more sincerity, *señorita*. But I can see you still hold me responsible for the thoughtlessness of my *amigos*.'

'I no longer consider it any of my business, *señor*,' Terry said. 'The old lady suffered no harm, nor have I. If I've thought about the incident at all it is merely to wonder how, when I warned the old woman in your own tongue, you were so quick to assume that I was English.'

It wouldn't have been true to say that he relaxed his arrogant bearing, but there was a trace of humour in his manner as he replied, 'There are many with your porcelain blue eyes and honey-brown hair in our country, *señorita*, but not one of them would toss crumbs to the fish on a hotel jetty with such tender affection.' As a form of farewell he took her hand and brushed the back of it lightly with his lips. 'I am happy to discover that you are unhurt. Perhaps we shall meet again.'

'I hardly think so. Will you be staying long at the Hotel Esperanza?'

He paused and his answer when it came was measured in some way. 'I shall be there for a little while yet, I think.'

Terry moved towards the doorway. 'Enjoy your holiday, *señor*. *Adios*.'

'*Buenas noches, señorita*.' For a moment she caught sight of his aristocratic bearing in the light from the house, then he had disappeared in the gloom. Moments later the backfiring of the decrepit van split the peace of the evening before it rattled away, eventually leaving everything as calm as before. Or so it seemed. Listening to her visitor's departure Terry felt a little unsettled at his '*Buenas noches*'. But she had supplied the correct hint of finality with her '*adios*', so that should be the end of that.

Supper was on the table when Verna arrived. Changing into a loose caftan for the meal, the older girl was full of what she had discovered during her outing. 'The town's full of gossip at the moment.' She helped herself to slices of ham. 'The Marqués can't make a move without the grapevine twitching. Apparently his girl-friend's arrived in Pollensa. There's pressure from his family in Madrid, it seems, to see him married and settled—as he's well into his thirties, I suppose—and by all accounts Miriam Perez is a stunner. Her father is a retired diplomatic official and as the Marqués was once himself a diplomat before going into business on the island, there's probably a close tie between the two. Anyway, it appears the Señorita Perez is a strong favourite among the Marqués' elders.'

Though all this was related with the usual detachment Terry got the idea that Verna was not pleased at this latest piece of gossip. Spooning extra sweet corn on to both their plates, she put in chattily, 'Do you think the Marqués will bend to his family's wishes and marry Señorita Perez?'

Verna smiled as though at some secret thought. 'I get the feeling that he's a man who intends to suit himself in these matters. According to his reputation, he's successful with women and there's no doubt he can take his pick, but in the end I think he'll choose his wife his own way, with or without the family consent.'

'Perhaps he's in love with Miriam Perez,' Terry said. 'Has no one thought of that?'

Verna's smile became fixed. 'I wouldn't think so.' She shrugged. 'Spanish marriages tend to be arranged . . . and in any case love, these days, can be a temporary thing.'

Terry didn't quite know what to make of her colleague's comments. She supposed it was natural that the Spaniard who had commissioned them to design the interior of his house should dominate their every conversation, and growing increasingly curious about him, she asked, 'Verna, what's he like—the Marqués?'

'Typical blue-blood,' came the reminiscent reply. 'By that I mean it shows in his manner, adds a kind of attraction, though he hardly needs it. He can be haughty when he likes, proud I suppose you'd call it. Like all aristocrats he's imperious too, though he has a way of teasing which softens any impression one might get that he's out to have his own way.'

Terry began to experience an odd sensation. *Well into his thirties*, Verna had said. She clarified her earlier question by adding faintly, 'But what does he look like—physically, I mean?'

'Haven't I told you?' Verna was surprised at the omission. She went reflective again. 'Everything about him is so compact and inured it's difficult to separate the looks from the man, as it were. I suppose you could say he's got an athletic build, but he's not beefy, more on the lean side. His features are typically Spanish—you know, the aquiline nose and flashing dark eyes, but his smile is international, you might say. When he turns it on you forget the arrogance of his breed. Oh, and his hair. He's got the most disgustingly luxuriant mop for a man, it's black and shiny and waves just enough to complement his olive skin.' Verna straightened. 'There! I think that just about sums up our current client. If you get the impression that he's a man difficult to ignore, that's the Marqués del Alcázar. Although,' she paused dreamily, 'his physical aspect is not nearly so interesting as his bank balance. He's very rich. Owns half the island, I believe, and several business concerns in Madrid. Can you imagine us landing a job with someone in his financial bracket!' Verna lapsed thoughtfully. 'There ought to be some opportunity to . . .'

But Terry wasn't listening. Something was bothering her. It was curiously tied up with the left-overs of sweet corn in the dish, and all that the older girl said after that came to her as though from a distance.

She didn't feed the fish on the hotel jetty the next morning. In fact she wasted no time at all in getting down to the supermarket in town. Alfredo was nowhere about, so she was compelled to go patiently through her shopping list around the deserted store. It was only when she was placing her order near the till for delivery that the store owner appeared, a little bleary-eyed, because of the early hour, perhaps.

Without bothering with pleasantries this morning she asked, 'Alfredo, who was the man in the store yesterday when the tins fell down?'

But this was beyond the storekeeper's comprehension of English. 'The man,' she emphasised, miming, 'who delivered our groceries last night?'

This time it registered. 'What could I do?' Alfredo's eyes bulged as though recalling that some rigid demands had been made. 'When someone like . . .' He stopped to eye her sceptically on thinking the matter out. 'You have had no introduction to Rafael de Quiso?'

'Yes, we've met . . .' Terry bit back her impatience. 'But is he known by another name . . .? I mean . . .'

'But of course!' Alfredo shrugged as though it was too early to have to explain what everybody knew. 'He is the Marqués del Alcázar.'

Terry had walked for a full ten minutes before she had brought her annoyance under control. Oh, very funny! The Marqués del Alcázar driving up in a wheezing store van to deliver her groceries! He must have enjoyed *that* joke. And even more her belief that he was a reckless holidaymaker seeing the sights with his friends!

But what ruffled her most was that while she had been in the dark regarding his true identity, he had known as soon as he had discovered her address at the supermarket who *she* was. He had provided the accommodation for her and Verna, so he would know who was installed in the cottage. She smiled cynically to herself. He probably owned it—and half the villas on the estate too!

She ought to have had some inkling, of course, as to his monumental status in the tiny community, having seen the old woman's startled reaction when such an eminent figure had actually enquired after the humble soul's well-being following the heavy fall of corn tins. And the way Alfredo had practically grovelled at his feet to gather them up afterwards. But how could she be expected to know that the very man she had clashed with in a disturbing way, and then practically froze on the spot with her attitude when he had visited her at the cottage, was none other than the one who had commissioned her and Verna to come to Spain to beautify his villa!

She went hot and cold when she thought of it, but it didn't ease her indignation. How dared he make pointed references to her 'career' and leave her to battle in the dark with such mystifying comments! How dared he bait her with obscure remarks about his love life and her own apparent lack of one, knowing she had no idea of the personal link that existed between them!

The fact that he had enjoyed himself at her expense made her seethe, but she had the consolation that she had been caustically exact in her dealings with him, which evened the score somewhat.

Her feet were taking her in a particular direction and it was only when her irritation had subsided that her plans to see the Marqués' villa for herself came through. Everybody knew that the magnificent new property perched at the tapering end of a ridge, with another mountain ridge and deep gorge behind it to give it a fitting dramatic position above the town, belonged to the Marqués del Alcázar. Verna and Terry had had it pointed out to them by townspeople almost from the moment of their arrival. They had been waiting for a direct introduction from the owner before making any approach, but Terry saw no reason for further delay. She at least had met him, if not formally, and she was filled with a mounting curiosity to see the house that she was expected, unknown to him, to transform.

The road to the approach was the one that flanked the rear of the hotel and Spanish villas along the sea-front, and which ran past the cottage and the white houses of the holiday estate north of the town. It was

little more than a country road taking merely the tourist cars and tripper coaches which made for the tortu-
ous mountain route to Formentor at the extreme tip of
the island, and she had it almost to herself as she
walked.

She arrived at the gateway leading to the villa and
might have been dissuaded from making the trip if her
determination to see what the Marqués had built for
himself in such dominating surroundings had not been
so strong. Certainly there was nothing inviting in the
long walk through flanking cypresses which must have
stretched for a mile or more up the slope towards the
hillside retreat silhouetted now in bright sunlight
against the shadowed gloom of the valley and ridge
behind.

The cypresses were centuries old and the impressive
route they lined must have belonged at one time to an
older historic dwelling. But it had a charm of its own,
the walk, and the trees made it shady and peaceful after
the noise of the port.

Terry took her time and at last came to a sharp
bend in the route leading to the right and then a
sharp left turn which was no doubt designed to take
in the steepness of the climb. Round the last bend
the villa came clearly into view. The layout was
spectacular. Open patios and blossom-draped courtyards were backed by the craggy backdrop of the
farther ridge, and matured gardens where everything
grew from masses of colourful flowers to stately palms
and banana trees convinced her that the site was an old
one indeed.

The roofs of Mediterranean red tiles were diverse
and covered with a variety of angles, which meant that
there was nothing three-up-and-three-down about the
Marqués residence. The interior was obviously intri-
cate and interesting and suggested alcoves and all the

touches which gave a house character. Its walls were of pink-hued stone. It had traditional arched doorways and grillework-screened windows, and through these she could see spacious rooms with gleaming ceramic-tiled floors.

They were completely devoid of even the simplest preliminary step towards furnishing, and all at once Terry was seized with a bout of panic. More than ever she hated the deceit that she had become enmeshed in regarding her work. But these were not just the familiar misgivings she had known in the past. It was the thought of the Marqués which unnerved her. Somehow she couldn't imagine him being lenient with someone who had tricked him, even in the mildest way.

She turned quickly away from the house and took a few steps into the grounds. The place was clearly deserted. The gardeners would work only in the cool of the evening, she guessed, and she could see the advantage now of such a setting; why no high walls or screens were needed to protect the gardens from the variable winds of winter. The ridges themselves offered vast protection, and the sun was so hot here on this sheltered platform that even the delicate banana palms flourished in its all-year-round warmth.

The whispered sigh of the breeze was all one could hear, here where the vast sweep of bay lay like azure silk, rucked at the edges against the white houses of the port, and the silence of its encircling mountains reverberated, it seemed, in this upper air.

It was a soothing spot to linger, but Terry felt neither soothed nor at ease as she hurried down to the road again. She hadn't liked the idea of coming to the island with Verna's schemes for creating false impressions, and now that she had met the Marqués she liked it even less. There was something oddly disconcerting

in the thought that she, and she alone, was going to
have to dream up interior comfort where a man like
Rafael de Quiso would live.

CHAPTER FOUR

TERRY felt too unsettled to return to the cottage and as it was still some way from lunchtime she wandered back to the port with a view to buying fresh fish for the meal. She could see the fishermen gutting and cleaning their morning catch in their boats tied up beside the big yachting marina across the road. But just when she was about to take advantage of a lull in the traffic a voice from a nearby café table made her hesitate. 'Well, if it isn't me old mate, Terry!'

She turned and her blue eyes widened at the sight of a familiar, rather delinquent figure in faded jeans and rough denim shirt sprawled in a chair beside a table. 'Leigh! Leigh Chandler! What on earth are you doing in Majorca?' she exclaimed with a laugh.

The young man with greasy, wheat-gold locks and darker gilt stubble on his chin pulled himself into a more upright position and indicated the chair beside him with a grin. 'Take a pew and I'll tell you the story of my life.'

'You forget—I know it,' she laughed again, thankfully accepting the seat after her long walk.

Laconically he attracted the attention of a waiter and ordered a drink for her in fluent Spanish, then he turned to meet her gaze with his usual idle irony.

Leigh was a long-standing friend of hers. He lived in a flat across from hers in Earl's Court. They had met for the first time, somewhat stormily, one Sunday morning about eighteen months ago when they had both insisted on having the last remaining paper at the corner news-stand. Terry had been adamant, claiming she had got there first, and Leigh had been equally unyielding, banking on his friendship with the newsvendor to give him priority. But the wily old Cockney, not wanting war on his hands, had promptly separated the newspaper into two equal parts, demanded half the price of it from each of them and told them to swop pages when they had read their fill.

It solved the problem, and when Leigh came across to call on her for the remaining sections of his newspaper they both began to see the funny side of it. Terry learned later, rather surprisingly because of his appearance, that he was the son of an eminent Harley Street surgeon. His rooms, when tidied up—a task that was often left to her—were elegantly furnished and in an exclusive block of apartments, but he conducted himself like a hippy and had no real settled employment.

He was a university graduate but hadn't followed up any kind of career and seemed to drift from one thing to another. He had a genuine interest in the outdoors and was clever with languages, and this had enabled him to secure the odd position as a courier abroad, or guide in some summer resort. But he never held a job for long, possibly because his appearance was against him, and certainly because he displayed no real interest in work of any kind.

Terry's friendship with Leigh had lessened since Verna had come on the scene. She had been too busy for their usual walks in the park or to sit in the local coffee bar for a chat. But she saw him occasionally and he knew that she had gone into partnership as an interior designer. Like everyone else he assumed that Verna was the creative member of the team. Terry had seen him just before she came away and had confided in him concerning the commission they had accepted to work for the Marqués del Alcázar.

Now his hazel eyes crinkled at the brightness of the Majorcan sunshine, and bursting with curiosity, Terry used an old joke between them to rouse him into an explanation. 'Well, don't keep me in suspenders. What *are* you doing here?'

'Simple,' he shrugged. 'The old man's terminated the lease on my digs at the end of the month. In layman's language—yours and mine—he's refused to fork out any more money for rent.'

'Oh, Leigh! I'm sorry.' Terry looked at him with genuine concern. 'What will you do now?'

'Sleeping on the Embankment would be no hardship,' he smiled bitterly, 'but the thought might offend my mother's taste.'

Terry was silent for a moment, then she asked, 'But how does that explain you being here in Pollensa?'

'To use a word that, as you know, doesn't often come into my vocabulary,' he grinned with delinquent pride, '*work!*—graft—stint—that's the reason I'm here. With news of the foreclosing on my lush living which I've fleeced my father for unashamedly for the past two years I've had to stir myself—get off my ... er ... tail and scan the Sits-vac columns. But I'm strictly an individ., and no smooth-talking travel agent is going to tell me what to do, so I latched on to the idea of supervising birdwatching groups myself. Maybe you don't know it, but Majorca is, *the* island for this kind of lark—sorry about that—and Pollensa especially abounds in the long-tailed, smooth-crested this and that, *plus* the bespectacled amateurs who plod around in knee-length shorts and hiking boots hoping to get a gander. My job is to round them up at any hotel and smooth the way for them with my well-oiled Spanish while we're out looking for their little feathered wonders.'

Terry had been thinking while she listened. Being

country-bred she knew something about birdwatchers'
habits, and it was this knowledge which made her
comment, 'But isn't May a little late for the sport over
here? I would have thought March and April were the
best months for migrants. And September–October at
the back end of the year.'

Leigh reached for his drink with a leisurely air before
replying. 'There's always something to be seen for the
birdwatching fanatic, and it's on the cards that the
bunches I round up will be happy enough searching
for the elusive miracle in the bushes.' He took a long
gulp of his beer, placed the schooner carefully on its
paper coaster and asked, 'How's it going with the
Marqués del Alcázar?'

Terry was mildly surprised to hear him refer to their
latest client by his official title. Leigh always ridiculed
pomp of any kind and used idiotic nicknames for
people in high places to display his contempt. But
obviously it hadn't occurred to him to do so in this
case.

'We're still waiting for a meeting,' she gave a shrug,
not caring to mention what she knew of the Marqués
herself. 'Apparently he's being very gentlemanly in
giving us plenty of time to find our feet on the island,
before putting us to work.'

'I've seen his palace among the crags.' This de-
rogatory comment was characteristic of Leigh, at least.

'Who hasn't?' she smiled. 'It's visible from most
parts of the town. As a matter of fact, I've just come
from a visit there. I went to take a look round on my
own and I must admit I'm very impressed. It's a dream
of a place.'

'He can afford it,' came the sardonic reply. 'Has a
finger in all kinds of business schemes, so I hear, and
makes a go of everything. Mind you, a guy with his
background can't go wrong anyway.'

'I'm sure it's not just his title that makes him successful,' Terry said evenly. 'There has to be some hard work somewhere behind his kind of achievement.'

'How would you know?' The observation was made derisively. 'You're just a skivvy waiting to do his bidding.'

'It's just a feeling I have.' Terry had a sharp vision in her mind of a man who was too keen-witted to be content in himself with past family glory.

'Sure! He's as energetic as the rest of us, and his Marquis of somewhere or other handle makes no difference at all.'

'The rest of us, did you say?' Nettled, though she didn't know why, at this constant knocking of a man she had met only briefly, Terry viewed the lank locks and unshaven chin of the younger figure across from her and remarked severely, 'You're an able-bodied individual yourself, Leigh Chandler. Why don't you put some of that university education to use and aim for similar heights?'

'Me?' Her companion put on a shocked smile. 'You know that kind of effort would be likely to kill me.'

Terry sighed. Not joking herself, she said shrewdly, 'Because your father's a brilliant heart surgeon it doesn't mean you should feel inhibited by his success.'

'I don't!' The young man shrugged innocently and unconvincingly. 'As all the psychiatrists will tell you, I just see myself as an acorn growing in the shade of the big oak tree.'

'But acorns get to be oak trees themselves one day,' Terry reasoned.

'Not all of them. A lot wither under the weight of the big cheese daddy oak in the background.'

Terry sighed again. It was useless trying to get Leigh to see that he was a prime example of wasted manhood. His father had tried often enough, she supposed, so what hope did she have, a mere friend, in getting him to change his ways? There was a small difference now, of course. He needed money now that his father had finally cut off his allowance. Why, she wondered, had he chosen Pollensa for the purposes of making a bid to stand on his own feet? She wouldn't have thought that the opportunities abounded in this tiny fishing port. Or anywhere else on the island for that matter. As for his birdwatching guided tours, this was something new for Leigh, Terry was sure, and she couldn't think how he hoped to survive for long financially on it.

While she was lost in her own thoughts the subject of their slight difference of opinion was clearly still very much on Leigh's mind, for taking another gulp of his drink and tightening his lips over the taste, he said, 'Anyway, just to put you right on what you think you're going to get in the way of a winsome Spanish patron, I've met your Marquis bloke, and to quote one of my lesser-used drawing-room expressions, he's a so-and-so.'

Terry put her glass down to stare at him. 'You've met the Marqués? How come?'

Leigh shifted his lounging frame and gave her a twisted smile. 'I haven't been sitting drinking hooch since my arrival in this one-horse village, you know. I've spent some time exploring and pumping the locals, and it's known that the valley lying directly between the Marqués' spanking new villa and the far ridge, known as Altramuz Valley, is the resting place for such marvels as blue rock thrushes, black vultures, gold-finches, falcons—you name it, it's likely to be there in the Altramuz Valley—means lupin, by the way—Unfortunately the whole damn stretch, some two miles to the sea, is owned by the Marqués, so I knew I'd need permission to take birdwatching groups there.' Leigh's smile became more warped. 'Oh, he agreed to see me; turned a polite blind eye to my "weird" appearance, even plied me with wine in typical fashion of Spanish hospitality and gave me some pointers on the Tucan Marsh bird life area over near Alcudia. But on Lupin Valley he was charmingly unshiftable. There were lots of walks, he said, without risking the litter of tourists in his backdoor woodland estate.'

Having heard this Terry shared her friend's disappointment. 'That's rotten luck, Leigh. But perhaps the other routes he mentioned will prove to be just as fruitful.'

'I've a feeling,' came the weighty reply, 'that at this time of the year Lupin Valley is the only place which will keep my birdwatching customers coming back for more.'

'I do hope you make a go of it,' Terry said sincerely.

Her words seemed to dispel some of her companion's disillusionment and taking her hand he smiled lopsidedly. 'It's like you to care when you've got a lot to think about yourself, Terry. You've always been a sweet kid. I don't know why you bother with a dropout like me.'

'Even drop-outs can have a certain appeal,' she twinkled.

He squeezed her fingers in a way that brought a warmth to her cheeks and asked, 'Will you come here to the Bar Fabula again some time?'

Terry thought about it and nodded. 'I expect to be very busy shortly, but I'll try and make it whenever I'm down this way.'

This seemed to satisfy Leigh, and finishing her drink she left him sprawling with one leg on the chair she had vacated, his hand raised in indolent salute.

For the return route she chose her favourite walk, and strolling past the inlets of shady pines and lapping translucent water she thought of Leigh with a warmth

and returning confidence. It was good to have someone
she knew close at hand. There was Verna, of course,
but her colleague had an insular nature and strangely,
though their work together created an intimacy between them, it had never overflowed beyond the bar-
riers of a business partnership. Whereas with Leigh
she could chatter on about inconsequential things and
laugh with him as one did when one felt totally at ease.
Yes, a new happiness filled her knowing that the young
man, the only one in her busy life since taking up
interior designing, was here on the island. There was
just one tiny question which persisted at the back of
her mind. Why had Leigh chosen Pollensa on the
island of Majorca to organise his birdwatching groups?
Was it just coincidence that it happened to be the ideal
spot for such a venture?

It was a morning filled with shocks of a differing
degree, and the greatest one of all was when she turned
into the cul-de-sac towards the cottage and saw a
familiar sports limousine parked outside on the road.
She had only seen the car once before, but she would
recognise its expensive lines anywhere.

Her heart began to bang against her ribs as she went
in the gate. She could hear voices in the living room
and slipped round to the kitchen entrance to strive for
more even breathing. So the Marqués had finally
decided to pay them a call, and by the sound of it he
had brought someone with him.

Terry smoothed her hair, brushed off her flower-
sprigged summer dress and went in as though meeting
Spanish noblemen formally was something which
happened every other day in her life.

The atmosphere in the living room was decidedly
informal and relaxed. Terry didn't know how Verna
did it. She was sitting, legs crossed, in an armchair,

looking for all the world as though she had expected
the visit, in tight black slacks and hip-length black and
gold caftan, her gleaming dark hair tumbling attrac-
tively around the boat-shaped neckline. By contrast the
woman in the opposite chair appeared overdressed in
an outfit cut on Paris lines. Her beauty too seemed a
little out of place in the rustic decor of the cottage
living room.

Her skin had the waxen pallor of a race that shuns
the sun, but none of the sallowness. Her black hair
glinted with the lacquered sheen of the true Spaniard
and she wore it not lustrously displayed as one would
have expected, but in a chignon which placed in relief
far more effectively the superb contours of her face.

Terry lingered over the woman's rather vapid smile
so that she could put off as long as possible acknow-
ledging the presence of the man in the room, but it
had to come in the end.

The Marqués had risen at her entrance, and as her
blue glance met his gaze she detected a touch of flinty
mockery in the dark depths. All right, she said silently
with her own look, so you're not a hell-raising holidaymaker, but I still think you acted like one playing
cheer-leader to your unruly friends, despite your
fancy title.

As Verna stirred herself to make the introductions
Terry thought she saw a slight hardening of that pleasant expression when her colleague said, 'We've been
hearing how you met the Marqués del Alcázar before
his scheduled visit to us, but I don't believe you know
his friend, Señorita Perez. This is my assistant, Miss
Teresa Heatherton.'

'Personally I think it is *muy comico*, you running into
Rafael in a supermarket of all places. *Realmente*, Raffy,
you do lower the tone of our society circle! And battl-
ing with tins of corn too? Why, it is like something out

of *el teatro comedia*. Tell me, Señorita Heatherton, how did you manage to turn on the ice so effectively, refusing to have anything to do with the stern overlord in these parts? You know you have laid yourself open to a very nasty bout of unforgiveness. Rafael does not let off lightly anyone who has made him angry; although it seems for the first time in his life he has met someone who couldn't care a fig either way!'

The shallow laughter and inane chatter issuing from such regal looks took one rather by surprise, but Terry managed to conceal hers and replied, 'Believe me, I had no idea I was tang!ing with the local aristocracy at the time.'

The Marqués offered her his chair and commented drily, 'I am convinced it would have made no difference to you if you had.'

So her look had gone home. She purposely avoided his gaze, but was very conscious of his presence in the room. He had lowered himself into an adjoining armchair and this simple action filled the air with a vibrancy, made it, for Terry at least, slightly suffocating.

She also sensed Verna's displeasure over something. She, Terry, had always remained in the background where clients were concerned, and she got the feeling now that Verna would have preferred her to perform a lightning exit after making the visitor's acquaintance. But the fact that the Marqués had presented her with a chair was making this difficult and without wishing to be she found herself the centre of attention because of the silly incident in the food store.

'It will be all round *Los salónes del elite* in no time,' Señorita Perez again, 'how Rafael was put in his place by a slip of an English girl.'

'I shall try to live it down,' came the suave reply. 'Though I admit it will be difficult when it is known that my adversary has such childlike habits as throwing breadcrumbs to the fish in our waters.'

Not that again!

Terry had the feeling that the Marqués was sparring with her in looks at least, unknown to the others, but she didn't give him the satisfaction of glancing his way in that moment.

'Oh, I like that!' Miriam Perez clapped her white hands in delight. 'The little fishing girl and the big bad nobleman. It is just too *encantador*!'

Terry could sense that Verna's teeth were grinding behind her smile at the woman's idiotic conversation and striving to extricate herself she said, 'I assure you I'm just a working girl and I've come to Majorca to do a job, not to become a legend as the only one who dared to cross the Marqués del Alcázar.'

She heard his low laugh at this, but there was the suggestion of steel in his voice as he replied, 'You have a lot to answer for, Miss Heatherton, but I shall seek atonement in my own way. In the meantime we are here to invite you to dine with us this evening, with your charming employer, of course, Miss Wendell.'

Verna took up the conversation smoothly. 'We'd be delighted, Marqués. We are not yet familiar with your place of residence, but . . .'

'I shall send someone to direct you,' he smiled across the room.' As you have probably discovered, we dine late in Spain. Shall we say nine-thirty, to allow for pre-dinner drinks?' There was no doubt that Verna was eager, but without waiting for a reply he nodded as though when he decided something there was no question of a refusal. '*Excelente*. We shall look forward to seeing you.'

He turned directly to Terry then and asked, 'Are you enjoying the beauties of our island, *señorita*?' There again was that look that took her back to last night's conversation when he had more or less accused her of paying too little attention to her surroundings.

'I'm captivated.' It wasn't her intention to sound sarcastic, though where the Marqués was concerned she was sorely tempted to.

As though he sensed the leaning that way he said, 'You have seen far beyond the fishing port here, of course?'

And of course he knew she hadn't. They had come here to work, not to do picnic tours around the beauty spots, but if she voiced her thoughts his eyes would suggest that she was being career-minded again. 'Does one need to go farther?' she said carefully. 'I'm sure Pollensa has everything, scenically at least, to keep the visitor content.'

'True, the bay is *magnifico*, but there is more to the island than its lovely coastline. We must organise an outing for our friends, Miriam. Show them that this fragment of Spain is truly what the holiday brochures claim it to be.'

Rafael was baiting her mercilessly, that much Terry knew. He wouldn't let her forget that she had frowned on the exuberance of his tourist friends. But he didn't know the barrier of reserve she had erected had been mainly a form of defence against his stringent charm.

'Oh, that will be *maravilloso, carino*! We will take them to the gorge at La Calobra, so *dramático*! And on the winding road to Formentor. Oh, I get so dizzy on those frightful bends, but it is so exciting, so spiced— is that the right word, Miss Heatherton?—with danger . . .!'

The frothy chat of Señorita Perez filled the room. Verna's expression remained pleasant. Her social finesse was unparalleled. It had been acquired over the past year, from the numerous parties she had attended in the course of business, and though she must have been itching to she made no mention of the Marqués' villa.

Maybe it was just as well, Terry mused privately, that she was not in charge of the situation. She was too outspoken to play these party games and would have come straight out with the reason why they were on the island, and what they were going to do about it. It irked her to have to await the Marqués' pleasure. Unlike Verna, she was not prepared to set aside her pride for the sake of business.

How much of her thoughts were discerned by the man reclining in the armchair she didn't know, but his next remark was addressed to Verna. 'Soon we shall have to think of giving your assistant something to do, Miss Wendell. Time appears to weigh heavily on her shoulders.'

'She is young and keen, Marqués,' Verna smiled. 'But I find her suitable for the help I require in my designing.'

'She is a little ambitious, this *ayudante* of yours,' Rafael de Quiso joked darkly. 'Perhaps she plans to steal some of your flair and be as successful as yourself in the art of interior design one day.'

Fortunately Señorita Perez rose at that moment. Clearly she was a woman who could sustain interest in a conversation for only so long, and undoubtedly now as the afternoon lunch-hour was approaching her thoughts were turning to food.

Terry took advantage of this signal of departure to rise too, and when she turned from replying to some comment the woman made about the garden the Marqués del Alcázar was bowing over Verna's hand and saying in urbane tones, 'I hope we have not put a stop to any creative thinking with our visit, Miss Wendell. Please do not disturb yourself to show us out. We look forward to seeing you this evening with your young aid, who I am sure will not mind now walking with us to the car.'

Did Terry have any choice in the matter? With such a man the answer was, no. She led the way to the outdoors and purposely took up more conversation with Señorita Perez to allow him to precede them along the drive. But curiously it was Miriam who appeared to be holding back for a word and when the Marqués was sufficiently out of earshot she said with a touch of relish in her voice, 'I think I had better warn you that Rafael is not a man to forget easily something which has made him angry. Do not be misled by his charm and his friendliness, *amiga mia*. It is a mask which hides a temperament of steel, and when he is at his most pleasant it is then you should be on your guard.'

'Thank you for telling me, Señorita Perez,' Terry smiled. 'But I don't expect I shall be seeing much of the Marqués during the course of my work.' Privately she hoped not. The more she saw of the Marqués del Alcázar the more she was convinced that Verna was playing a dangerous game in deceiving him.

The man of her thoughts assisted Miriam Perez into the car. He came round the rear way to the driving seat and said to Terry in the gateway, 'Until this evening, Miss Heatherton. You are looking forward to dining with us, no?'

Had he guessed that that was the last thing she wanted to do? She met his penetrating glance and replied, 'If the invitation is meant to make up for the thoughtlessness of your friends, you could have saved yourself the trouble, *señor*. I have long since forgotten the incident.'

His smile did not reach his eyes. With a hard whimsy there he made the brief gesture of a bow. 'Whereas I am known for my tenacious memory, *señorita*. *Adios y gracias*.'

'Thank you for what, *señor*?' she raised her chin enquiringly.

'For accompanying us to the gate, *naturalmente*!' With the obscure remark he got into the car and drove smoothly away.

Terry turned to walk back up the drive, allowing herself one glance behind as she did so, in time to see the white car, the Marqués at the wheel, just turning out of sight. Out of sight, out of mind, she decided firmly, and concentrated on the bemusing impact that Señorita Perez had made with her visit. She went indoors, expecting to share with Verna some amused perplexity that a woman with such an arresting face could have so little behind it. But she soon saw that anything so lighthearted was far from her colleague's mind in that moment.

It wasn't that Verna looked very different. Her expression was still pleasant, but it was drawn tight across her features so that it appeared almost brittle. She hadn't risen from her chair and from there she asked, 'Why didn't you tell me about the episode at Alfredo's?'

'It was too silly to mention,' Terry shrugged. 'One never expects pyramids in grocery stores to collapse, but this one did, and . . . well, there's little more to it than that.'

'Do you think it was fair to leave me to hear it from the Marqués himself what happened, and to sit here and watch the two of you exchanging subtle messages with your looks?'

Terry didn't explain that the Marqués' visit last night in the delivery van was at the root of their silent sparring match. She said, 'I'm sorry, Verna. If I'd known it was the Marqués del Alcázar, our patron, that I'd run into in the supermarket I would certainly have mentioned it. Anyway, it seems to have broken the ice and we've made his acquaintance formally at last.'

'Don't rush to the conclusion,' Verna said with a tart smile, 'that your close call with the tin cans had anything to do with Rafael's visit here today. Naturally he's a man who would show concern for anyone involved in an accident, but we do have the commission to fit out his villa, and that's most likely the reason for his calling today.'

Most likely. Terry didn't mention either that the Marqués had already called to check up on her physical state the previous evening. Recalling the invitation to dinner, she said, 'I know you don't care for the idea of me attending a function which is mainly for business, Verna, and quite frankly nor do I. I'm sure I could cry off; think of some excuse . . .'

'In this case I think not, Terry,' Verna cut in. She rose, the brittle pleasantness more apparent than ever, and moving in the direction of her own room added, 'As my "assistant" naturally you form part of the team the Marqués has engaged for the work on his villa, and he'll expect to see you there in this capacity at least. I suggest you put on something pretty and do your best to impress where you can, with a view to more business. But one thing we should get straight from the start.' Verna's smile was taut and calculating. 'Keep your charm for the guests, pet. Rafael is *my* department.'

CHAPTER FIVE

TERRY couldn't settle to anything during the afternoon. The unease she felt at Verna's blithe determination to go through with their duplicity despite the risk of working in so intimate a community as this island hamlet was growing inside her. She wished there was someone she could talk to, thought of Leigh with a sudden glow, then recalled that he had troubles of his own at the moment and would be more inclined to be looking for a sympathetic ear rather than offering one. But later, when he had got himself organised as guide for birdwatching groups, she might confide in him; see what suggestions he had for extricating herself from an alliance which had seemed harmless enough at the beginning but now was getting frighteningly out of hand.

In the dusk she wandered about the garden, doubly aware of the scents of oleander and jasmine and the perfumed leaves of geranium, perhaps because her nerves were overwound; or was it because she recalled a certain figure standing about here last night ... autocratic white smile and dark eyes glowing in the shadows.

Because of a tightness around her heart she would have preferred no more meetings with the Marqués del Alcázar, but despite its warning messages something in her would not be stifled at the thought of seeing him again, if only for this one introductory dinner.

Rafael de Quiso sent an official car to collect the two girls from the cottage. It was black and sleek and roomy and smelled of the endless succession of distinguished personages that the chauffeur must have ferried back and forth in it at the Marqués' pleasure. Because of its size and splendour one would have expected a journey of considerable duration, which was why Terry, at least, was surprised to find that after a few minutes along the *avenida* leading to the sea, the limousine drew to a stop between the beach terrace and the low-walled area fronting the Hotel Esperanza.

At this time of the evening the interior exuded an elegance with its subdued coppery lighting, the grand cedarwood pillars and mellow Spanish furnishings of the huge lounge, shining warmly through the big picture windows. On the other side of the impressive doorway the garden-side restaurant was crowded and animated in a discreet way, maroon-jacketed waiters gliding between the tables with typical Spanish detachment.

As the chauffeur was holding the car door for them Terry saw nothing for it but to alight. Verna, who had never been known to let any emotion register on her shrewd features, stepped out with her usual smile, and as she did so Rafael de Quiso came out of the doorway to meet them.

The backcloth of luxury suited him. In dinner jacket he appeared darkly attractive, his manner more urbane than ever as he brushed Verna's wrist with his lips. '*Bienvenida*, Miss Wendell. I am happy that Fernando has delivered you to my doorstep without mishap . . . Miss Heatherton,' his black gleam took in Terry momentarily and she had a feeling that his comment was meant cryptically for her. But it was the 'my doorstep' bit which caused her to wonder. As though he was aware of this he put a hand under Verna's elbow. 'Shall we go in?'

Traversing the carpeted foyer towards the lift, he

explained with a quirk of roguish amusement about his lips, again for Terry's benefit she didn't doubt, 'Until the Villa Al Azhar is completed I am, alas, without a roof over my head, so temporarily I am using the top suite of the hotel. It is close to the villa and the town and suits my needs perfectly.'

Leaving the lift, he showed them along a private corridor and through a doorway where a party of sorts was obviously in progress. 'Merely business acquaintances,' he assured them as a valet and maid came forward to take their wraps. 'I have many friends internationally and the hotel is accustomed to housing them frequently, but tonight all will be seriousness and calm.'

Terry looked for some means of escape. Any more innuendoes and Verna would be bound to link his teasing with herself. As it happened, the scene of Spanish graciousness was enough to claim her attention for the next few minutes. If this was a hotel suite nobody would have guessed it from the fine old tapestries and wall-hangings, the Alfonso reign period furniture and crested carpets reminiscent of an old and grand Madrid.

Silver-framed ancestors in sepia photos and silver serving bowls and goblets glinted on velvet-draped tables. Hinting at adventure, there were crossed swords on the walls and pricelses antiques going back to Spanish seafaring days. But far from appearing grand and intimidating, the room was given an atmosphere of cosy intimacy by the glow from ruby red droplets circling the crystal chandeliers.

In this softened light it was easy to see that the Marqués had chosen his temporary lair well. All around through the undraped picture windows was the spangled view of the bay, the radiant star-flecked sky framing the winking illuminations of its coastal surround and a mountain loveliness that night only enhanced.

Rafael introduced them to the other guests; couples and individuals who made little impression on Terry's mind. They were mainly Spanish and their names would have defied repeating anyway, but it was an acute awareness of Rafael, suave, at ease and commanding in a subtle way that had nothing to do with looks, which dimmed every other presence in the room for Terry.

Verna stayed with her for some moments, suspecting perhaps lack of confidence in her tongue-tied attitude. Behind her smile she said in low tones, 'Some of these people I've seen at the parties in London. They won't bite you, you know. Just behave normally. They'll understand that you're here only in the capacity of an assistant and will expect little from you.'

Well, that was a relief, Terry thought wryly. In a dress of spring green gathered closely at her waist and tiered in broad frills to just below her knees, she didn't suppose she was going to attract too much attention. But that was because she was unaware of the youthful glow that lit her features or how it gave her a simple beauty among all this sophistication.

'One thing you can be sure of,' her colleague was saying still beneath her breath, 'Rafael doesn't entertain snobs.'

And Verna would know, Terry mused privately, aware of the other girl's experience at such gatherings. That experience which she wore like an enamel, but which curiously didn't detract from her womanly appeal. She certainly looked striking tonight in a rather bizarre white suit with gold tasselled epaulettes at the shoulders and similar fringe round the skirt hem. She believed in dressing outlandishly, did Verna, to suit the part, and she looked every inch the eccentric interior designer.

It was obvious too that her eyes were following Rafael as he circulated among his guests. Terry couldn't deny that her own glance had hovered for most of the time in that direction, although she was not fool enough to believe that the charming smile that hovered about his lips now was the true measure of his character. She had seen that he had a temper, if controlled, that he could be arrogant and imperious, and to recall last evening that he could also be mocking. But was this even entirely the man? What of his romantic life? What quickened his blood where women were concerned? That conquests among the opposite sex would come easily to such a man was more than apparent, but to what depths did his affections go? Was he capable of deep love, or were all his affairs merely the pursuits of a virile man?

Heavens! Terry pulled herself up sharply. What was happening to her thoughts? Decidedly getting out of hand, yet she was reluctant to alter their course. And what of Miriam Perez? Would the Marqués be content to overlook her vapid charms for the purposes of possessing her beauty physically and domestically in marriage? Anything was possible, Terry told herself, and Miriam must be one of the loveliest women in Spain. She was here tonight, bare-shouldered and quietly dazzling in black. Her trite laughter could be heard above the talk of the other guests.

When she had sized up the room herself Verna steered Terry towards pleasant company and left her with the advice, 'Just act naturally, and remember, you're here simply as an underling in the business.'

At ten the guests sat down to dinner. Terry was made to feel at home by the attentiveness of her immediate neighbours; a smiling matron on the one side with a heavy emerald crucifix resting in the well of her ample bosom and a wraith-like gentleman on the other side whom everybody addressed as *el Conde*.

Even so Terry was hardly aware of what she ate. This was altogether new to her and she had never seen how Verna would shine on these occasions. Seated next to the Marqués with Miriam at his other side, her colleague was entirely at ease, and without appearing to work at it secured the attention of most of those seated at the table as she related her experiences at some of the top residences in London.

Later they moved to a balconied lounge for coffee. Terry was seated on a settee, having been propelled there by a big-boned woman with reddish hair. Miriam was in the midst of an admiring group. Verna and Rafael were talking in low tones together in a corner. 'You are thrilled to make this trip abroad with your enchanting chief, Miss Wendell?' Señora Carra, wife of a Madrid businessman, questioned her with bright-eyed interest.

Terry smiled. 'It's a lovely island and I'm enjoying my stay here very much.

'You are fortunate to have such a talented *maestra*.' Broad hands were clasped across a satin-clad middle. 'I have seen some of her work in London and I can understand Rafael's eagerness to put her to work on his villa.' The *señora*'s glance searched out the pair in question in their corner and with a naughty gleam she added, 'They have got something—what do you say—going, those two. I have never seen the Marqués so engrossed.'

Terry put in lightly, 'I've heard it said that Señorita Perez is the woman in the Marqués' life.'

'All of Spain knows that, *querida mia*.'

'Yet one could hardly call her possessive.'

There was a deep shrug. 'Miriam is like the island *mariposas*. She is happiest sharing her beauty with her admirers, as the butterfly prefers to flit from flower to flower. But in the end she will marry Rafael, *sin duda*.'

'How can you be so sure, *señora*, if Señorita Perez is easy on the matter . . .?'

'*Ajá!*' A hard chuckle from the older woman. 'I can see you have not heard of *la madre*.' Señora Carra leaned closer as though in confidence. 'Miriam Perez possesses *un pariente*, *un matriâca* with a will of *hierro*—iron-minded, you would say—Both families are agreed that the match would be perfect, the mother most of all, and when Doña Otero Perez decides on something everyone knows that it will be precisely so. Even the Marqués has a certain respect for *la madre*.'

Terry could believe it. Spanish traditions went deep and arranged marriages tended to be a success. Also it did seem that Miriam was well suited to the grandee style of living.

Her thoughts were interrupted by a powerful sense of awareness. She felt rather than saw that Rafael was making his way over. Verna came with him, She and Señora Carra were clearly well acquainted, for without preamble the older woman said, 'I've been thinking of what you told me about silver and ice-blue, Miss Wendell. My salon would look magnificent as you described it, but a little cold, I think.'

'Then the answer is a touch of deeper blue here and there, or even a dash of royal purple,' Verna replied with complete aplomb. 'I always encourage my clients to be colour mavericks when it comes to their choice of decor.'

'We have not got your imagination, Miss Wendell,' Señora Carra said with a smile. 'But you always manage to make what sounds *alarmamente* look adorable when the designing is under your supervision.'

Regarding imagination it was as well that not too many were blessed with it, Terry thought privately.

Deep purple with ice blue and silver would be horrific!

'What is your opinion, Rafael?' Señora Carra turned to him. 'You have seen my *salón* often enough, would you say——'

The Marqués put up a hand. 'Miss Wendell is the expert on decor here, Margarita. I trust her judgment so completely I am leaving the entire interior of the Villa Al Azhar in her hands. If you have a problem concerning your *salón* I suggest you discuss it to the full with Miss Wendell. In the meantime, as everyone else appears to be well occupied, I shall take her young assistant to view her favourite sport—that is, to see the fish from the jetty——'

'In the dark?' Verna's smile was sharply pleasant.

'The fish are pets of the hotel,' Rafael lifted his shoulders lightly. 'They enjoy the beachside illuminations almost as much as we do.'

Terry felt stiff and strained as she went out with him. In his evening attire, sartorially correct, he was a little formidable, and it was almost as though he had planned this moment from the start; his bringing her out here tonight was more like a command than an invitation.

Of course there were no fish to be seen from the sailing jetty at this hour, as she had known there wouldn't be, but the view was magnificent, the lights of the coastal night-life appearing almost full circle round the bay.

From where she stood with him on the jetty Terry said, still unbending, 'It's a lovely panorama.'

'We are blessed with entrancing sights here in Majorca,' Rafael replied, also cool. 'But I did not bring you out here to seek praise. I simply wished for a word with you alone. You are angry because I played my little joke on you with Alfredo's delivery conveyance, is that not so?'

Terry shrugged. 'If a Marqués of some standing in the nobility wishes to amuse himself playing errand boy locally, I don't see that it's any business of mine.'

'But you would have preferred that I did not try to lighten your mood with a little nonsense. Or perhaps you are piqued to learn that I am to be your *dueño*, your master in the matter of the Villa Al Azhar and your work there?'

'As I see little of the people who engage ... Miss Wendell, I hardly think it matters, do you?'

'Perhaps not. Certainly you have not displayed much pleasure in the dinner party I arranged for you tonight. I suspect you would have avoided the invitation if that had been possible, *no es verdad*?'

Terry felt too keyed up to answer at once. It was true she had in a way dreaded another meeting with Rafael, sensing that her busy, well-ordered life could not support someone so emotionally disturbing. It was as well to know one's place in this life, and as an assistant, or so everyone thought, she knew it was better that Rafael remained the Marqués del Alcázar and she a figure in the background. That way she would be spared, she knew, a draining experience that she could well do without, on top of what she was already having to cope with.

'If you want the truth I would have preferred to stay away,' she spoke at last. 'The feeling that you included me in the party because you felt you had to after what happened——'

'You will not tell me how and why I issue an invitation,' he cut her off, his eyes black and hard. 'I merely wish to know why you are not at ease under my roof tonight. You have spoken little to the guests and appear poised for flight most of the time.'

Terry chose her words carefully. 'I am not acccustomed to attending these functions, *señor*. I have a job to do, and working with Miss Wendell I'm not often called upon to shine at conversation.'

'Are you trying to tell me that your employer would not wish you to feel relaxed on such an occasion? That I can hardly believe, *señorita*. Miss Wendell is a charming and benevolent *maestra*—much more forbearing, I can assure you, than the ones we have in Spain.'

Terry felt she was getting in too deep to continue, therefore she remained silent. This did not please Rafael either and with a flicker of impatience he took her arm. 'Come, we will walk awhile. Perhaps then you will forget about employers and work and we shall see a glimpse of the girl known as Teresa wrapped in all that assistant prickliness.'

Terry had no choice but to accompany him. His fingers on her arm were warm and firm and they steered her off the jetty and along the path fronting the hotel. But when he stopped at the dark shape of an entrance to an adjoining property she tensed and asked, 'Where are you taking me?'

Rafael chose a key from one of the many on a gold chain and inserting it in the lock of the huge old timber gate he replied, 'You have seen my temporary quarters at the hotel. Now I will show you the more permanent one of my island ancestors.'

They entered an area steeped in gloom and choked with low-growing palms and trailing blossom. But the white structure of the hotel nearby offered some respite from the pitch-black night, and holding her arm impersonally Rafael guided her along an overgrown path to the shallow curved steps of an arched doorway.

Another key, another eerie creaking in the shadows and they were engulfed in another kind of darkness until her escort found a switch and some faint illumination sprang to life. It was the yellowish light Terry had seen in the old mansions along the beach path, emitting from bulbs whose electric glow appeared in some way to have mellowed to blend in with the antiquity of its surroundings. Of course she knew it was just dated installations, but to her artistic mind it was a fitting inadequacy, for the brilliant white lights of, say, the seaside apartments would have been almost irreverent here.

They were in a stone-floored ante-room with a central stairway winding upwards. Faded heraldic brocades hung on the walls, a time-worn figure clothed in a suit of armour and visor graced an alcove and the windows were narrow slits built, it seemed, rather for protection than beauty. Terry was interested, she couldn't deny it, and sensing the leap in her Rafael led her to a doorway which opened on to a cloistered courtyard. Even with only the aid of the starlight she could make out its symmetry and crumbling perfection. High in the open archways of its surround doves flapped and cooed as they must have done centuries before, and tall graceful pepper trees softened the worn stonework with their foliage.

In such a place Terry felt uneasy beside Rafael. But, in no hurry to continue the tour, he said, 'The family home has not been considered habitable for some time, though I lived here until the Esperanza was completed two years ago.'

She must have shown some of her wonderment, for he smiled without warmth and remarked, 'You are surprised that the Esperanza is so youthful? Most visitors believe it to be a relic of the days of gracious living, and that is the effect I wished to create. The Quiso manor, as you can see, is filled with old ghosts and anything brash alongside would have been unthinkable. But the grounds with their own outlook to the sea were too beautiful to lie hidden with time, so the Esperanza was a means of sharing some of our island charm with visitors.'

'That's very generous of you,' Terry said politely. She kept the colour out of her cheeks with some effort, recalling how she had reprimanded him for hogging all the jetty with his friends. No wonder he had displayed steely amusement. He *owned* the jetty, *and* the hotel!

And of course the stately old palms and pines which gave the Esperanza its mature loveliness had once graced the garden of the old manor; an asset that Rafael had been astute enough to recognise.

At the moment his attitude was wholly austere. 'Your tones imply that I am merely being condescending,' he said harshly, 'in my wish to share what I possess with others. But that is because you do not understand the deep significance of a family name such as mine, and one's desire to perpetuate its renown. Your young mind is no doubt centred on today and those who people our present existence ... especially certain young men in *el puerto*.' Rafael measured a trumpet blossom, which trailed nearby, across the palm of his hand and asked, 'When did you first meet Leigh Chandler?'

Terry fought to hide her surprise at the question. 'I've known him for the past eighteen months or so,' she replied noncommittally. 'He lives close to me in London.'

'A state of affairs which required slight rectification with your move out of here.' After this obscure remark the Marqués added, 'I do not think it is good policy, Miss Heatherton, to allow yourself to be seen with the scrofulous young Chandler. The Bar Fabula is the most popular café in the port. Its tables also happen to be on view to all who pass by.'

Meaning to say that he had seen her there with Leigh

while driving by, of course. Anger rising in her, Terry replied, 'I'm not troubled by appearances, *señor*. Leigh may not be very prepossessing, but he's a friend of mine, and I don't think my associating with him will be too damaging to your image, considering that I'm to work for you at your villa.'

'You insist on reading *mal intencion* in everything I say, *señorita*.' The Marqués' eyes narrowed, showing irritation and shrewd distaste. 'And the speed with which you rush to the defence of the young misfit countryman of yours is touching. Could it be that he is the one who will in the end thaw a way through the work-bound casing of your heart?'

'I'm not in love with him, if that's what you mean,' Terry said flatly. 'But nor do I turn my back on him simply because he doesn't conform to the accepted standards of dress and behaviour.'

'Very noble.' Those expressive lips were shaped in a sneer. 'And what do you base such tender loyalty on? Young Chandler's—what do you say—track record so far?' When Terry didn't reply he went on, 'It may surprise you to hear that I too know something of your young friend's background. He has been in the port only a short while, but already he has established his habits over here. He is known to be over-fond of drink, sleeps through most of the time and associates freely with drug offenders.'

'Like all those who pride themselves on being adult,' Terry scorned, 'you're not interested in understanding the problems of the boy. All you can see is that he's not like you and millions of other upright, clear-sighted men.' She took a breath. 'No one is prepared to understand that Leigh has an oversized inferiority complex. His father——'

'Sir Hugh Chandler,' Rafael nodded implacably. 'I know of him and of his fame as a Harley Street specialist, and he has my sympathy. When I have sons they will not be permitted to become wastrels.'

'They wouldn't dare develop a success complex with you for a father,' Terry retorted in barbed tones.

'They will be given the upbringing that I myself was given. Is there anything wrong with me?'

'A little less inflexibility wouldn't be out of place,' she dared to suggest. And going even further, 'I think it's mean of you, not allowing Leigh to take his bird-watching groups into Lupin Valley. Perhaps you think he might contaminate the wild life there with his un-disciplined ways?'

'Contamination is an ugly word, Miss Heatherton.' The Marqués gave her a straight look. 'But yes, I do feel that Chandler's presence would be all wrong for the tranquillity of Lupin Valley, as you call it, and I intend to stick to my refusal of allowing him free movement there.'

'It will ruin his chances to make a go of his guided tours,' Terry exclaimed resentfully. 'He's got to earn money somehow.'

'Then we must see what else can be done. If his survival on the island is so important to you, we must certainly see what can be done.' Almost roughly Rafael gripped her arm to move on again, but stopped as they turned towards the doorway to add, 'Just one more thing, Miss Heatherton. Why did *el chico* Chandler follow you here to Majorca?'

'I don't know that he did follow me here.' Terry shrugged off the question. 'It was just coincidence that the island, and Pollensa in particular, happens to be one of the best birdwatching areas in the Mediterranean.'

'So that is what you think, *señorita. Vaya!* You are more *ingenua* than I suspected!'

Impersonally he took her on a guided tour of the

upstairs apartments, pointing out items of interest as a warder would have done showing a visitor round a castle.

The island mansion was incredibly old, appearing to date back to the first settling of Rafael's ancestors in the thirteenth century. There were ancient broadswords on the walls, shields and daggers, and the lighting of those far-off days were wooden cartwheel-like fixtures hanging chandelier fashion in every room, each fitted with a circle of ironwork candle-holders.

Fourposter beds graced the sleeping apartments as well as oversized rocking chairs, china dolls in greying calico, and in one corner of the main bedroom a wedding dress yellowing with age was draped in a glass case. Fascinated by this relic of a happy moment in some woman's life, Terry was drawn to studying the seed pearls sewn into the fabric, and noting how the material was rotting around each bright stone she felt choked with emotion at the sadness of the passage of time coupled with the lingering nostalgia of a ceremony that is eternal.

'It is the dress of a long-gone *pariente* of mine.' Before she had time to recover herself Rafael was beside her. 'Luciana was my mother's great-grandmother. She was married at eighteen and had seven children.'

Terry looked through the arched windows at the starlit view of sea and gardens and said with feeling, 'She must have been very happy here.'

The Marqués replied with mild irony, 'Marriages were an embodiment of twin spirits and enduring in those days.'

Terry tried to sound offhand. 'But it's no different for you now, surely? I thought in Spain of all places, deep-seated traditions remained.'

Rafael shrugged. 'Progress must be heeded and because of it we are catching up rapidly with the rest of the world. With new laws on permissiveness and the lowering of morals we cannot wait to join the race to self-destruction.'

Terry afforded herself a smile. 'Your outlook for the human race is somewhat cynical, *señor*.'

'Evil destroys, *señorita*. Goodness is our only salvation on this earth.'

A profound thought. Or could it be that he was harking back to Leigh again?

She said with a show of making light of the theme, 'I'm sure goodness will prevail in the end.'

'It is possible.' His gaze was on her as he spoke. The dark pupils of his eyes seemed luminous in the skyglow. Because she was acutely conscious of their deep-searching almost ruthless discernment she said quickly turning, 'What is this?'

The silver-based crystal container was the first object she could find to touch. As though aware of her sidetracking the moment Rafael smiled dryly. 'It was the custom in those days,' he said,' to keep as a memento a little of the baptismal water of the first son. The liquid—of which traces may still be seen in this vessel—anointed Alejandro, Luciana's firstborn.'

Thinking of Miriam Perez, Terry asked, 'Shall you uphold such traditions, *senor*?'

'My son will be a Quiso,' came the clipped reply. 'Naturally I will do all in my power to ensure that he is aware of his birthright.' With this he escorted her from the room.

Downstairs he showed her bookcases filled with handwritten volumes and yellowing documents. In the vast kitchen iron implements decorated the huge stone fireplace. The smell of decay was in their nostrils and the Marqués told her, 'You are witnessing a bygone era, *señorita*. Everything concerning the past here is

being prepared and in a few months' time the house
will be opened as a museum.'

'Won't you miss the Quiso ghosts at your new home
on the ridge?' Terry ventured to ask.

'The Villa Al Azhar is built on the site of a domain
which belonged to a long-dead relative of mine. I have
retained the old name, but there will be no family heir-
looms there.' The hard mouth sloped. 'Like you, Miss
Heatherton, in some ways I prefer to live in the present.'

'It's a lovely construction,' Terry said. 'I took the
liberty of walking up there to take a look round.'
Without consciously working at it she had already
devised some unique schemes in her mind for the
rooms.

'Do not be misled by the apparent blandness of our
May sunshine.' The Marqués spoke sternly. 'You
could do yourself harm wandering along the uphill
route which was never intended to be negotiated on
foot. But tell me, what are you ideas on the Villa Al
Azhar?'

All too aware that this was dangerous ground, Terry
replied briefly, 'Architecturally I find it intriguing.
The interior, of course, will be up to Miss Wendell.'

'And will you follow her instructions implicitly?' he
asked.

'That is my job, *señor*,' she answered.

'But is it not possible that some small fraction of
your own personality will manifest itself in such
work?'

'Following the edicts of the master, *señor*, that is
hardly likely.' Speaking from a dry throat, Terry perhaps put the wrong slant on her replies, for the
Marqués said with a disapproving smile,

'You resent your employer's versatility, yet you
should be proud to work with her. Miss Wendell has a

gift for creating harmony and beauty in a home at no sacrifice to comfort; a gift which is becoming lost in the bizarre creations her so-called fellow professionals are producing these days in the name of art. That is why I chose her to take charge of the Villa Al Azhar's decor.'

Terry knew a secret thrill that the Marqués liked her work, but it was laced with a misery at having to conform to the deceit woven long ago and now like a web of chains about her.

She changed the subject to enquire, 'And your friends Señorita Perez—does she too like the Villa Al Azhar?'

It was almost certain that having seen Terry chatting with the outrageous gossip Señora Raffa earlier, the Marqués would have guessed that the subject of their conversation was his expected betrothal to the Spanish beauty. But giving nothing away in his expression he said merely, 'Miriam has not yet been on a tour of the new construction. I have forbidden her to view the villa until the interior is complete.'

Was he planning to present it to her as a surprise on their wedding day? Terry wondered. 'She's a very beautiful woman,' she said sincerely.

'The most beautiful woman in Spain,' he replied.

Feeling a little bleak, Terry asked, 'May we go now, señor?'

'You have found the tour of the old house overwhelming, no?'

It wasn't only the Marqués' family home that was overwhelming! 'It is full of history, señor. Who wouldn't be impressed?' she returned in a low voice.

'But with your mind fixed on the present and the economic survival of your young friend Chandler you find it difficult to appreciate the past glories of an ancestral home.' With this curt statement he led her outdoors.

The lights out, the great doors locked again, they were back in the deep gloom of the garden. Terry hurried along, intent on showing Rafael that she needed no assistance in the darkness. But her knowledge of the route was not as clear-cut as she was striving to make out and, losing her foot in a water channel that cut across the path, she lurched violently. Any man would have come to a girl's assistance in such a situation, but the way Rafael saved her set Terry's heart thudding against her ribs. With his arm about her waist he not only kept her upright, but pressed her to him as though it was necessary for the steadying of her limbs to be held close against him in this way.

For a moment she saw his white teeth displayed in an unpleasant smile, glimpsed pinpoints of something like anger in his dark eyes. Was he annoyed because she hadn't been more enthusiastic about his family relics? If not, what was the reason for his almost punishing grip on her? Perhaps he was teasing her again in an oblique way, displaying his Latin charm, his sophistication where women were concerned.

She wondered, in that close embrace, if he could feel the leaping of her pulses through the thinness of her dress; wondered too if he was amused inwardly at the nervous quivering of her limbs, the uneven sound of her breathing.

Wouldn't any woman, she told herself weakly, be conscious of his powerful male attraction? That indescribable magnetism which some men possessed, and which Rafael wielded effortlessly by simply a touch. Yet his hold on her indicated strength and deep undercurrents of something that showed as saturnine mastery on his face.

Some feminine instinct warned her to run from him,

at least mentally, keeping her emotions intact. But far stronger than this was a desire to press closer to him, to keep the moment endless, terrifying and exciting as it was.

He let her go abruptly while she was clinging to the last vestiges of resistance. 'Those who look at the stars must remember to keep their feet out of the gutter.' His deliberate twisting of an old proverb matched the satirical slant of his smile. For a moment the air remained unbreathable, for Terry at least, then with a hand under her elbow he escorted her impersonally through the gate.

Upstairs in the Marqués' hotel suite the rest of the evening passed in something of a haze for Terry. She was aware of Verna's probing glances from time to time and worked to put on a look of complete indifference at being asked to accompany Rafael out of doors. But inwardly she knew that something shone in her, a blazing radiance that would have to be quelled somehow. She couldn't be in love with Rafael? Such a thought was too devastating to consider. He was a Spanish *marqués*. And she ... well, what was she to the world? No more than a decorator's assistant.

CHAPTER SIX

THOUGH thoughts of the dinner party at the hotel suite remained in Terry's mind for long enough afterwards Verna made no direct reference to the occasion except to point out that the way was now clear to begin work on the villa. Businesslike as always, she was keen to set into motion plans for transforming the interiors. Only this time Terry sensed a not so subtle difference in her colleague's approach. That Verna was out to impress Rafael as they had never impressed before was apparent in the almost feverish way she tackled the situation.

'I want the best you've got in that neat little brainbox of yours, Terry, for this one,' she said, pacing the living room the next day. 'Now that the social niceties have been performed, Spanish style, we've got a free hand with Al Azhar, and I won't settle for anything less than perfection, understand?'

'You mean we're at liberty now to wander round the place as it suits us?' The panic rising in her, Terry hedged with the kind of remark that usually taxed Verna's patience.

'Why do you think Rafael invited me to his hotel suite last night?' she asked with a hint of exasperation. 'That's the way we do things in the decorating business. He and I had a long and useful talk and really got to know one another, and the outcome, my pet, is that he has given me a set of keys so that we can come and go as we please.'

'In that case,' Terry said morosely, 'I suppose you'll be wanting to take a drive up there?'

'I can see,' commented Verna with a sour attempt at a joke, 'that it was a mistake to leave you to your own devices. You've got so used to dreaming your way around the port you seem to have entirely forgotten that I've landed you one of the plummiest commissions you're ever likely to get. We'll start out straight after lunch,' she added in her decisive way. 'And let's hope the meal will give you a little more enthusiasm for the job!'

The drive between the columns of ancient cypresses filled Terry with a curious sense of peace. In the afternoon heat a haze hung over the countryside and far from the growing clamour of the beaches and port she felt soothed and oddly comforted by the sight of the lone house on the ridge. As they alighted from the car the only sounds to be heard were the lazy whirring of crickets in the undergrowth and slumbrous drone of insects on the warm air.

Verna cast a cursory look around, then went to the main entrance, keys in hand. Inside the echoing emptiness of the rooms, the sunlight filtering through here and there, Terry knew a need to be alone; to give herself entirely to the feel and dimension of each interior, not, as Verna supposed, searching for inspiration, but because her mind was filled with pictures of Rafael, one day, dwelling here. There was nothing at the moment but walls and roofs, but it was strange how, to her, his personality was already ingrained here; in fluted pillars and concave ceilings; a circular window framing hot blue sky and Spanish terrain.

After two or three days of wandering through the villa she found the ideas started to come. Lost now to the realisation that she and Verna were partners in deceit, she found the urge to create something worthwhile out of bareness and austerity ruled her so completely she thought of nothing else.

'This second *salón* is easy,' she said musingly to

Verna, standing by with a notebook and pencil one day. 'Its smaller windows and intimate size will allow for a cosy but elegant arrangement.' She surveyed the white ceiling-to-floor fireplace with its tapering chimneypiece and knee-high hearth. 'We'll keep it pure white just as it is,' she announced confidently, 'and the walls on either side we'll have a cool, clear green which will accentuate its smooth lines. A pair of green Venetian glass candlesticks, I think, for the ivory mantelpiece, and twin silver lamp brackets, one on each green wall, with ivory silk lampshades ... The rest of the room panels will be green with doorway woodwork and skirting boards picked out broadly in white.'

She eyed the floor, like some of those in the other rooms, awaiting decoration, and mentioned, 'There's a deeper green tile I've seen. It's got a brilliant gloss and a small yellow square in one corner which when laid gives just the right relief to the overall green ... this would be broken up by white fur scatter-rugs ... Twin sofas flanking the fireplace are a must, daffodil silk I think, with sprigs of green, and to add a Spanish touch, a couple of circular tables one in either corner of the walls framing the fireplace, with typical floor-length curtains, of course ...'

Verna had a hard, pleased light in her eyes while she scribbled rapidly. She was shrewd enough to recognise artistry when it was explained to her.

Sometimes she left Terry on her own to browse through the rooms, dropping her off at the villa in the afternoons and going on to report, as she called it, to Rafael on their progress. Terry had no need to ask what happened on these sessions with the Marqués. That Verna was reeling off the ideas to date to him as though they were her own was obvious—and necessary, Terry supposed glumly, if they were to see this thing through without mishap.

But apart from these attacks of conscience Terry loved being on her own at the Villa Al Azhar. Sketch-pad in hand plus the numerous swatches of the latest curtain materials and upholstery leathers, and nearby piles of glass and porcelain sales literature which Verna kept her stocked with, she was finding it immensely satisfying bringing a house to life.

Sometimes when she had pinned down a particularly elusive snippet of inspiration she would take a breather out of doors. Her favourite spot was on an elevated patio where twin pillars supported an arched lookout which framed the mountains and countryside above the little white houses of the port. Here she would listen to the singing of the breeze across the foothills below the ridge and the contrasting stillness of Lupin Valley in the shadows.

The fact that she was entirely alone and well removed from the populated sections of Pollensa gave her no cause for concern. Not until one afternoon when a movement in the bushes close to the lookout suggested that the presence there was something other than a bird.

Terry felt a fluttering of nerves somewhere in the region of her throat; a sensation that was instantly dispelled when a jean-clad figure with unshaven chin appeared. 'Leigh!' she gasped, laughing. 'You gave me a scare! What are you doing hiding there?'

'I've been waiting to make sure you're alone.' Showing no amusement himself, he came on to the paved patio. 'I want to talk to you.'

She knew a sudden spasm of worry and looked around before turning to him. 'You shouldn't have come here. I'm supposed to be working, you know.' She forced a lightness into her tones that she didn't feel. Leigh's sudden appearance seemed to darken the sunlight in some way, and the air that she had been quietly rejoicing in now seemed oppressive. It was his mood, of course, she told herself. Leigh was given to black depressions and they always had this effect on her whenever he was near.

'Does all right for himself, the old Marqués, doesn't he?' The young man idled around viewing marble tiles and carve stonework with a twist to his smile.

'I think you'll find that everything here is the result of his own endeavours,' Terry said evenly. Then, striving to remain pleasant, she asked, 'What did you want to talk to me about, Leigh?'

'We're already on the subject,' came the dry reply. 'Seems Rafael not only runs the port but has a go at organising people's lives as well.' At Terry's puzzled look he grinned mirthlessly, 'I didn't tell you, did I? He picked me up the other night in his racy Porsche and took me for a run along the coast. I thought he was hinting broadly that I should take myself over to the salt-flats to do my birdwatching stunts. But it was nothing like that.'

'No?' Terry put in enquiringly.

'No. It was much worse.' Leigh's grin disappeared in the gilt hairs of his beard. 'He offered me a job. Said that there was a position as receptionist going at a hotel he controls in Marbella. He said that with my language ability and university degree it would be a piece of cake—Well, being a Spaniard he didn't actually use those words, but something to that effect. Of course, he said, I'd have to clean myself up a bit— pinstriped trousers and black jacket were a must in a job like that. But Marbella, he pointed out, is a trendy tourist town and there'd be lots of free time to do my own thing, as it were——'

'Oh, Leigh!' Terry burst in at last. 'That's wonderful! It could be the chance you've been waiting for.'

'I thought you'd like the idea.'

The sarcasm in the comment pulled Terry up short. She looked at him and asked, 'Don't you?'

Leigh shrugged, but his eyes were hard. 'Does anyone want to lose his own identity? Besides, Marbella's about five hundred kilometres away on the mainland.'

'I'll admit it's a bit of a cheek interfering in your affairs, and suggesting you go all that way,' Terry considered. Then, enthusing again, 'But it would be the making of you, Leigh. There's no telling what opportunities could stem from——' Seeing that she was up against his grim withdrawal, she sighed inwardly and asked, 'What did you tell him?'

'I told him I'd think about it.'

'Oh, Leigh! At least you haven't turned it down. Will you truly think about it?'

'Sure . . . this year . . . and next year.'

'Oh Leigh!' Exasperation made her want to shake him, but she smiled instead with despair.

Indifferent to her mood, he resumed his idling, touching expert workmanship here and there with a shabby plimsolled foot. 'Let's just say,' he said after some time had elapsed, 'that for the moment I like it here in Pollensa.' There was something about the quirk of his mouth as he looked around that Terry couldn't fathom. But when he glanced her way she thought she knew the reason, especially as he added, 'After all, you're here. And when a guy's favourite chick is around it can make a whole lot of difference to the way he thinks.'

Terry smiled, though behind it she was a little suprised. It must be the Majorcan air or something turning Leigh's thoughts to romance. He had never been what one might call over-affectionate in England, but since their meeting on the island his feelings towards her seemed to have heightened in some way.

'I'm glad we met up like this,' she replied genuinely. 'It's nice to have a friend close by when you're working in a strange place abroad.'

'A friend?' Leigh crooked an eyebrow while moving in. 'I hope I'm more than that to you now, Terry . . . it's been almost two years . . .'

Terry was uncomfortably aware that he intended to take her into his arms. Either the move was too sudden after the brief acquaintanceship on the island, or it just didn't feel right. She wasn't sure which, but to offset the gesture she put out both her hands to receive him.

With a wry gleam Leigh clasped them in his own. It was only then that Terry woke up to the fact that a car had just parked on the paved platform beside the house. One part of her mind had heard its approach up the incline, but all of her concentration had been on handling Leigh without hurting his feelings. Now she heard the car door being closed discreetly and alarm gripped her as she told Leigh, 'You must go at once. Verna will be annoyed if she knows I've been wasting time talking to you.'

But some sixth sense warned her that it wasn't Verna, and turning, she caught sight of Rafael approaching the main entrance. That he had seen her and Leigh, hands clasped, framed in the lookout archway on his arrival she was miserably convinced—doubly so when he turned in that moment to bow their way and call, '*Buenas tardes*, Señorito Chandler . . . Miss Heatherton. I trust the view meets with your approval?'

Though she had fully expected it Leigh showed none of his usual swaggering bravado. Instead he gave her a quick nod of farewell and disappeared the way he had come in the shrubbery down the hillside.

Terry returned to her sketches and swatches indoors,

but ostensibly now with the air of following instructions laid down for the interior layout of the villa rather than issuing them. Rafael toured the rooms, his footsteps echoing on the bare floors and penetrating into the centre of her brain. Though she strove to ignore him every part of her was painfully tuned to his presence nearby. The tension would not have been so unbearable if he had made some comment, impersonal of course, concerning the 'duties' she was carrying out, but he merely circled her from time to time as he passed through to another room making calculations of his own.

She had got her breathing going shakily again, schooled her hands into working with barely a tremble, when he stopped on one of his tours and strolled over to view a sample of chintz she was making notes on for a file. 'The colours of *otoño*,' he said, fingering the design, 'or autumn, as you would say, are sometimes good for a house. I have often wondered what would be the effect if one had a room for each season; a spring room, dominantly green, of course; the summer one a full-blown yellow-gold, I think. Autumn mellow, and *invierno* red and cosy.'

'An intriguing idea, *señor*,' Terry remarked, not fooled by his seasoned smile. With a man like Rafael one didn't need facial expressions to indicate a mood which was in this case chilly and laced with contempt. His very personality made it powerfully apparent. 'I should talk to Miss Wendell about it,' she added carefully. 'I ... don't know whether it would ... fit in with her schemes ...'

'But I am just a novice,' he shrugged. 'And in any case I trust Verna's judgment implicitly. She is the artistic one, with a touch of genius that steals up on one unexpectedly at times. Do you not agree?'

'Yes,' said Terry in constricted tones.

'Your reply lacks sincerity, *señorita*. I sometimes think you do not fully appreciate the talents of your *maestra*. Or perhaps you are a little envious, no?'

'That's the second time you've accused me of professional jealousy, *señor*.' Terry dared to look at him, knowing that he was being deliberately malicious but not fully comprehending why. 'Even in a joking way,' she spoke over the commotion inside her, 'I fail to see why you should gather that impression.'

'In this example I would say a display of divided loyalties.' Momentarily his dark eyes glittered, though his charm almost came through. 'You are here for the express purpose of assisting your employer, no? Yet because she is not around to supervise your movements your enthusiasm for her efforts here is set aside for other more rewarding pursuits.'

Terry felt her cheeks grow hot. So he had to get round to it in the end. 'If you're referring,' she said, 'to the breather I was taking just now on the patio, that's common in England. Some of your employees in Spain may still do a seven-hour stretch without a break, but I for one have no intention of conforming to your antiquated ways.'

'All will be remedied in time,' he said thinly. 'But I doubt even then if the rules will allow amorous exchanges with the opposite sex, on the job.'

He hadn't mentioned Leigh by name, nor did she as she returned, 'If one construes *amor* in every gesture, *señor*, segregation will be the only answer for Spain's work-force.'

'At the moment I'm concerned only with results under my own roof.' His smile was hardly amused. '*And loyalties*. Discounting the fact that I as your *dueño* until this villa is completed, rate some such respect, do you think it is fair to Miss Wendell, who has been good enough to take you on as an apprentice, to make dates with port riff-raff, leaving her to assume that you are conscienciously engrossed?'

Terry felt emotionally in shreds from his rapier-like small talk. Being tied up inside in an endless muddle of half-truths and deceit left her tonguetied too. Tonguetied, crushed and unhappy.

Luckily the sound of the hired car engine saved her from having to make a reply. Hearing it come to a halt outside the villa, Terry deduced that Verna must have arranged to meet Rafael here.

The older girl came in with an air of brisk efficiency. Rafael had gone out to greet her and beside him she said, a message in her eyes, 'I hope you've got my notes written up, Terry. I want to give the Marqués a detailed description of my ideas so far.'

A wryness behind her expression, Terry gave a nod which said there was no need to worry, she knew her place in the presence of the Marqués. Leafing through her office pile, she handed the necessary notepad to Verna and on the tour of the rooms remained silently in the background while the other two talked.

Dressed for the part in white safari suit and purple bow-tie blouse, Verna would wave an arm now and again descriptively. 'I thought we'd have wood-panelling here . . . and in this alcove shelf a Louis Quinze sculpture, if we can get one.'

Hearing her own creative highlights being mouthed by Verna, Terry trailed round her mind tending to wander on to other things. It was only when they were in the smaller *salón* that she came to with something of a shock after she had heard Verna explaining grandly, 'I love this Spanish fireplace and I've decided to do the walls on either side a deep midnight blue. We'll have blue Venetian glass candlesticks on the white mantlepiece, white satin lampshades around the blue walls and glossy blue tiles for the floor . . .'

Terry listened wincingly. So Verna was having a go at impressing her own identity on the interior of the villa. But midnight blue for this room, no, no, no!

Rafael mused for some time on their surroundings, then with his voice full of charm he commented, 'Verna, as always your taste is superb and all of the varying degrees of shade I agree with. But of the choice of colour, no. Dark blue is of the night and this is essentially a daytime room. Daytime where all reflections are green. Yes, that is the colour I see it, a clear, fresh *verde*.'

'Just as you say Rafael.' Verna gave in equably, her eyes not quite meeting Terry's. The younger girl experienced only happy relief. Spring green had been her choice too. It was funny how Rafael's seasonal ideas for the rooms had been unfolding in her mind from the start, without her being consciously aware of it.

After that Terry got the feeling that Verna was irritated by her presence, and sure enough, a few minutes later she told her, 'You can pack up here now, child. I want you to pick up the post in town. I'm expecting those linen wall covering samples any day now. Take my car. I'm sure the Marqués will be kind enough to drive me back when we've finished here.'

'Nothing would delight me more.' His eyes dark with warmth, Rafael gave her his customary bow.

CHAPTER SEVEN

FOR almost a week Terry was spared further contact with Rafael. In his eyes the one creating the furnishing schemes, Verna, relegated her to menial tasks like collecting parcels which must be signed for at the main post office at the port, and telephoning through to Barcelona or London to see if various materials were available.

Privately in the cottage she worked constantly on plans and sketches knowing that Verna, closeted with Rafael at the villa, was airing them with her usual panache as though she had dreamed them up the night before.

This didn't bother Terry much. She felt too unsettled and despondent to care about anything. Sometimes when she wasn't working she would go for her favourite walk along the beach path. In the evening the view was particularly lovely with the bay's twinkling lights, but invariably her gaze would turn inland to the dark old structure of the Quiso ancestral home. Up there under the broad eaves in the main tower she could see the window of the bridal bedroom where she had stood with Rafael. The memory was imprinted on her heart, but each time she found herself reliving the moments she had spent with him in the old manor, she reminded herself that he would probably be amused if he knew.

She had no desire to be in Verna's shoes mapping out the layout of the villa with him, but she did feel a little wistful when she thought of Verna's constant nearness to Rafael; a nearness that was putting a firm new brightness in her partner's eye, by the day.

But though Terry had lost her zest for living there were compensations of a sort. And one was the arrival of the tourist summer on the island; days of golden warmth, gaiety and colour. Now the tiny beaches under the pines were decked with straw-thatched parasols and June holidaymakers romped in the sea with everything from inflated plastic boats to streamlined ski-craft and sturdy canoes.

A daily dip was now the order of the day with the growing heat, and in a neat swimsuit Terry found a trip to the beach in the siesta period something of a tonic for her tired spirits. The strips of sand fronting the hotel were minute, though there was a spacious corner adjoining the terrace and pleasantly shaded with tamarisks. However, this tended to fill up rather quickly with the overspill of hotel guests preferring the sand, so Terry chose a quiet spot at the far end of the crescent-shaped stretch away from most of the activity.

She loved the feel of the sparkling water on her skin. It was still cool enough to be refreshing, and watching the shoals of tiny fish dart from her passage kept her mind reasonably distracted. There were other distractions, of course. On the thin ribbon of sand separating her from the hotel section all kinds of small sailing craft took off into the waves. This stretch of coastline never became crowded with holidaymakers, but there were those who preferred its quiet beauty and charm, and it was here where Terry became acquainted with Yves and Pierre and the gallantry that could only belong to the French race.

Yves was short, fortyish, but with a superb athletic build. His friend was taller, older and athletic too in a gentler way. Neither could speak a word of English, but both would contrive to raise their sunhats whenever Terry appeared. Their courteous *Bonjours* were very eloquent, their friendly smiles irresistible. Terry could stumble along in French having done fairly well with it in high school. Yves was eager to show her the rudiments of windsurfing, something she smilingly declined. She learned that he had been three times water-ski champion in his seaside home town in France. He was excellent too at windsurfing. His friend Pierre was less practised but just as keen to demonstrate to her how much he knew. In fact they were just like small boys eager to show off in front of an audience.

But Terry liked them tremendously. They made her feel very special with their gallant greetings. She would watch them raise their sails, ostensibly with a view to 'putting in a little practice', but clearly for her benefit, and then zip out to sea if the breeze was fresh enough. Sometimes Pierre would take a tumble from his float, or Yves would have to let his sail drop in conflicting wind currents, then Terry's gaze would be discreetly turned in another direction.

After a strenuous twenty minutes they would return to oil up their magnificent suntanned bodies, and laze away the time on the sand. They told her they had rented a villa on the holiday estate for the whole of June. They were obviously wealthy, because they came to the beach each day in a magnificent gold estate car which they parked at the side of the hotel. No mention was made of wives—Terry would smile at the thought with amusement—but she gathered that the ladies were passing the time in their own way back in the seaside town in France.

These breaks at the beach would help her to cope with the drained feeling inside her, but once back at the cottage, her sketches spread out before her, the dismal mood would quickly take over. Her mind would involuntarily conjure up the image of Rafael and she would wonder how his courtship was progressing with the beautiful Miriam and what his opinions were of Verna.

She was hardly likely to discover the answer to the latter, yet she sensed something in the air each evening when the older girl returned to the cottage. The sharpness in Verna's expression remained, but there was an odd glow about her which had something of the effect of mellowing it, if only slightly. Little was said on the subject of the villa, and as her partner had never been one for small talk Terry was left to herself most of the time at the cottage.

Then things came to a head one afternoon when Verna returned to pack a bag. Terry had just got back from a swim and seeing the open travelling bag on the bed she stopped on the way to her own room.

'Rafael has asked me to go with him to Madrid to choose some of the furnishings for the villa,' Verna said briskly, tossing items of clothing on the bed. 'I hope the lists you've made are fairly clear-cut and easy to follow.'

'I think you'll find the descriptions adequate, and the trade names I've included will be your main guideline,' Terry nodded, her footsteps dragging. 'I'll get them for you.'

'No, wait!' Verna stopped her with a gesture. 'You can do that later. I want to talk to you.' That feverish sheen from some inner excitement made her features almost glisten as she spoke. 'This is not just another job to me, Terry. This is something much, much more important to me. I think Rafael likes me. He's been quite attentive this past week. And of course, as you've probably guessed by now, I'm in love with him . . .'

She stopped as though to let this last bit sink in. Terry said in her forthright way, 'You've never struck me as the kind of girl who would fall in love with her client. Are you sure you're not confusing the emotion with the fact that Rafael is titled, rich and successful?'

Verna gave her a straight look. 'I might be, but the picture's the same. I'm going to marry Rafael. He's the man, I know, whose life I want to share. I'm sorry, Terry. It means the end of a successful partnership, but you've got to understand I've been waiting for something like this. As the Marquésa del Alcázar I reckon I can say my ambitions have been more than gratified.'

A little sickened by Verna's businesslike manner, Terry put in, 'Aren't you forgetting Miriam Perez? The whole of Pollensa, as does Madrid, I believe, considers the Marqués' marriage to Señorita Perez a cut-and-dried affair.'

'If you knew Rafael as I know him,' Verna gave her a sharp smile, 'you would realise he doesn't care twopence for family pressure. Raffy!' Ridiculing Miriam's pet name for the Marqués, Verna tilted a mocking eyebrow. 'Do you honestly think the competition there has me worried?'

She's a very lovely creature, Terry could have said, but she refrained. After all, Verna was a keen businesswoman and if it came to a contest where Rafael was concerned brains might easily outweigh beauty.

Terry's lack of response in no way undermined the older girl's supreme confidence. She tossed a last item into the bag, zipped it up and standing it upright beside the door said, 'Well, that's the set-up. Sorry if it's been a bit of a shock.'

It was not a shock, Terry told herself bleakly. Verna's designs where Rafael were concerned were hardly unexpected. It was the rawness inside that was unbearable, having to listen to a declaration of love when she was trying to school her own heart away from such thoughts. Knowing that Verna was speaking from a partnership point of view she replied nevertheless, 'You needn't have bothered to confide in me.'

'Why not? We still have this job to do together. Besides,' going to titivate at the mirror, Verna turned momentarily, 'I'm counting on you to help me get what I want.'

Terry felt her legs go weak. 'If Rafael has invited you to go to Madrid with him,' she said quietly, 'I don't see that you need much support.'

'You know what I mean.' The reply was made with impatience. 'This is a semi-business trip, after all.— Later there'll be lots of ways you can influence Rafael off the side with flattering talk about me—my abilities, which we both know are legion, my prowess at parties—things like that.'

'Shouldn't love be a little less . . . factual?'

'In my book it's assets that count.' Verna searched for cosmetics in her handbag. Smoothing bright scarlet over her thin lips, she added, 'If you've any appreciation of all I've done for you in the past, you'll do this one thing for me.'

'I hardly think it's up to me,' said Terry from a dry throat. 'But I'll do what I can.'

'I'm glad to hear it.' There was no gratitude in the tones, just bland acceptance which gave way to a faintly mysterious note as Verna tacked on, 'Then who knows, I may be able to do something for you.'

Terry had no idea what she meant by this. Waiting, she heard the other girl say somewhat coyly, 'You didn't tell me Leigh Chandler was here in Pollensa.'

Verna knew Leigh from Terry's association with him in London. She replied steadily, 'I didn't know myself until a few days ago. He's here to act as guide for bird-watching tours in the district.'

'Is that the yarn he's spreading around?' Verna

viewed Terry sceptically. Then snapping her handbag shut, she said, 'I saw him leaving the villa down the hillside that day when I drove up to meet Rafael there. I must say I didn't know that things had hotted up to this stage between you, and if you've invited him out here for some clandestine affair—heaven knows he's not fit to be seen with in the more populated sections of society——'

'You've got it wrong—It's not like that at all——'

'*Let me finish.*' Verna's smile and tone of voice were bitingly decisive. 'As I was saying, what you do in that direction is your own concern, but I think I ought to point that as I'm the senior partner in this set-up and in charge of conduct at the villa, it will naturally be up to me to demonstrate the correct measure of authority by frowning on any such meetings while I'm around . . .'

For a moment Terry couldn't believe her ears. In the past Verna had only acted the part of the designer, but now she really believed she was in full charge of production at the villa, despite the fact that Terry was the one who was actually doing the creative work. And not only that. Verna also saw herself now as the one to give the orders and to be obeyed. It was strange what the prospects of riches and comfort would do to a woman.

A little numb, she heard her colleague continuing, '. . . But as I mentioned earlier, you bang the drum for me a bit, put in a good word for me with Rafael, and I'll turn a blind eye to whatever you get up to with Chandler when you're on your own at the villa.'

Terry was too incredulous and filled with revulsion to make any coherent reply. When she could speak evenly she said with a weary glance at her watch, 'What time is the plane? Shouldn't you be on your way?'

'We're leaving from the hotel in about half an hour.

I'll leave the car parked outside the entrance. You can use it for your sessions at the villa. And Terry,' Verna picked up her bag and advanced with a piercing look, 'I don't have to stress how important it is to me for you to give of your best in everything concerning the decor at the villa. Rafael's pleasure and complete satisfaction with the finished result will contribute greatly to my attraction as his future wife.'

With the semblance of a nod Terry got her the lists she required and went with her to the front door. But before she opened it she asked dully, 'Verna, what are you going to do if one day Rafael discovers the truth . . . about the interior of the villa?'

'That creatively I've had nothing at all to do with its layout or design? Or of those of past commissions in London from where he's gathered his recommendations?' Verna's face became pinched and wax-like as she mouthed the words. 'Do you think I haven't thought of that often these past nights?' An agonised look flitted across the calculating features and with her free hand she grasped Terry's arm. 'Rafael believes I'm responsible for all those original and talked-about interiors of his society friends. He also attributes all those scintillating ideas you've been producing for his future home to me—But that's something between the two of us, isn't it, Terry? And Rafael must never know, you understand?' Her face white with intensity, Verna snapped, 'Never!'

On her own Terry spent much of her time at the Villa Al Azhar. From the beginning she had felt an affinity with the tremendous peace of its surroundings—the twin craggy ridges, the sloping foothills sweeping down to the sea. And now that she was alone the ideas sparkled in her mind and she knew that what she was getting down on paper surpassed anything she had so far accomplished in the way of interior design.

Verna would be pleased, she thought dismally from time to time. For as her colleague had neatly explained, the more brilliant the execution of the decor at the villa, the more attractive would be her chances of becoming Rafael's wife. Verna wouldn't understand that neither she nor any other physical force could influence Terry's visions on how Al Azhar would look when it was completed. She worked from within and lived with that inner fire which was wanting to give of one's best for the sake of one's own ideals. In other words, what she did with colour and fabric in the rooms of the villa was by nature something she had to do; like a snake sloughing its skin, she thought with doleful humour.

It was on her third day at the villa that she heard a sound in the hillside shrubbery from an open window and tensed. Leigh again! She would really have to be firm with him this time and tell him not to visit her here. Besides, his mode of paying her a call was creepy, to say the least. Why did he always have to come via the undergrowth as though his appearance warranted such behaviour?

She went out on to the paved patio where only the breeze stirred, with a feeling of being an accomplice in something. At the arched lookout she was just about to call out crossly when a figure—not at all the one she had expected—came into view.

'*Buenos dias, señorita.*' Rafael was dressed in hiking slacks and open-necked shirt. He held a silver-topped walking stick in one hand. 'As you can see,' he said with a hint of mockery in his tones, 'I too prefer the rugged approach on occasion.'

Because her heart was thumping at his unexpected appearance Terry asked baldly, 'Where's Verna? I thought you were both in Madrid.'

'Miss Wendell had to go to London,' he explained

obligingly. 'There was difficulty with some of the items she has on her list and your own city, she felt, would offer larger scope in this respect. Naturally I prefer to remain close to the villa while it is in its early stages of preparation, therefore I returned on the morning flight from Madrid and arrived in time for the traditional *merienda*.'

That was the light snack taken around eleven on the island, Terry worked out in her mind, and it was not quite twelve now, so clearly Rafael had wasted no time in checking up on her at Al Azhar.

She was sure that her face must look drained from the swirl of emotion taking place within her, and turning away she spoke civilly. 'Well, if you'll excuse me, *señor*, I'll get back to work.'

As she had half expected, he followed her indoors, but not to make some comment on her present occupation, which was jotting down the floor dimensions of a window recess. Instead, pacing, he asked, 'Does it absorb you so much, your career? Are you content always with the shell of an unlived-in domain? Surely your *maestra* has explained to you the importance of viewing the outside of your work sphere; the surroundings which will, in the end, contribute greatly to its prime completion. *No es así?*'

How often Terry had gazed at the wondrous views and been influenced by them in her designing. But she couldn't say that now. Instead she replied woodenly, 'I'm aware of the scenery, *señor*. But my job is mainly measurements and fittings, and I can't do these sitting in the grass.'

'No, but you can find the right mood for your tasks.' His smile was insistent. 'That is why I am here to suggest a tour of the estate.'

'I seem to recall,' Terry said, 'that the last time you were here, you all but accused me of slacking.'

'Precisely, and now I am proposing that you come on a walk through *el valle de los altramuces* with me. But am I not the Marqués del Alcázar? And am I not also the ultimate authority here at the villa? For these reasons, if for nothing else, you will not refuse me, *señorita*.'

Tight-lipped, Terry saw that in his autocratic way he had a point. In jeans and sandals and cool sleeveless top she couldn't even put forward the excuse that she was ill-clad for the expedition.

His arm indicated the way and she preceded him with a sinking heart to the outdoors. He guided her along a route she had known nothing about until this moment. Following a winding path that started at the rear of the house grounds, they were soon ascending the lip of the nearest ridge. The air still had a pre-noon sparkle and Terry was prompted to say stoically, 'At least the morning is the best time to go on a hike.'

'Of course. I wanted you to make the trip before you became too tired with your work.'

Concern from him was the last thing she wanted if she was to remain in control of her feelings, and more than a little coldly she replied, 'You think of everything, *señor*.'

Rafael's fingers tightened on her arm. 'You are finding it hard to be pleasant, Miss Heatherton. Your attitude is somewhat . . . I think the word is starchy.' As they turned to survey the villa courtyards and paved patios spread out below them he added, 'Perhaps you are annoyed because it was I who appeared at the lovers' archway and not Chandler as you had expected.'

The Marqués could always be relied upon to speak his mind . . . sooner or later. Terry smiled grimly to herself. She had expected Leigh, but not as he believed for romantic motives. Not that it would change the picture, she answered, 'I haven't seen him since the day he called here when you drove up.'

'No, but *claramente* he is not out of your thoughts.'

'Naturally one thinks of someone who is in difficulties. Leigh has no money and nowhere to live. It can't be easy for him when ... when——'

'When I have prevented him from making an easy penny by flooding *el valle de los altramuces* with gullible tourists?'

'Birdwatchers are hardly tourists,' Terry maintained. 'Theirs is a very serious pastime, almost a dedication.'

'And what of your friend's dedication to supporting himself? He appears to have very little of that. I suppose you know of the position I have offered him; how I plan to dispatch him to Marbella on the mainland. He will have told you all about that, and no doubt you agree with him that it is not a good idea?'

At this Terry raised her chin. 'I agree with him that it's none of your business how he conducts his life.'

'*Pero tu si.* You prefer to feel responsible for him as one would a motherless child. You want to live the anguish of his every mistake, his every weakness even though you are powerless to change him. *Maldita sea!* Guidance for the young should be left to those who have the maturity to make a demand stick.'

'And what would you demand? That he turns angelic overnight? What you fail to understand is that Leigh has a very real problem——'

'His only problem, *señorita*,' the Marqués cut in, 'is one that is not uncommon among children with brilliant parents these days. They are brought up to believe that everything is instant, even success. And because they are not prepared to spend the years it takes to acquire the exalted position their elders enjoy they seek notoriety in other ways, mainly in weird behaviour and dress.'

'Perhaps you ought to add another title to your string of interests, *señor*,' Terry smiled thinly, 'That of psychiatry.'

'We have Mission houses in Madrid, *señorita*. I have talked to the boys there on occasion.'

Sobered by this remark, Terry allowed him to lead her on. The path took them round the very tip of the sloping ridge. At one side they could see the red roofs and pink walls of the Villa Al Azhar some way below, and on the other the dip of valley between theirs and the far towering ridge. Misty still, and gilded by the morning sun, it stretched, a sweep of sylvan quietude to where a wedge of blue sea was visible in the distance. That birds found it a paradise here was more than evident in the lush greenery and tremendous solitude of the place.

The descent was far from treacherous, but it was an overgrown path and Terry was obliged to rely on Rafael's assistance from time to time. She sought desperately to retain her mood of resentment as an armour against his nearness. It wouldn't do to let the Marqués del Alcázar know that Miss Wendall's misguided young 'assistant' had to steel herself against trembling at his every touch. Especially as he considered this no more than a contribution to her education while she worked at the villa.

Almost on the floor of the valley they came to a freshwater spring a few feet below. Rafael stopped, checked Terry with a hand on her arm and listening said softly, 'Wait. Soon we may see something of interest.'

There in the leafy stillness, his fingers warm on her skin, Terry was sure he must feel the throbbing of her pulses. Though he appeared to be intent on surveying the immediate woodland, more than once she felt his dark gaze lower her way. Studiously, in the heart-pounding silence, she kept her own on the sun-dappled greenery. Then suddenly a flash of blue, the colour of an evening sky, lit up the emerald shadows.

'There!' Rafael's arm came around her waist to steady her on the slope, which in her flush of discovery she had forgotten. 'One of the valley's resident blue rock thrushes,' he whispered against her ear as it alighted on a rocky outcrop beside the spring. 'And there too is the female coming in to weigh up the terrain.'

Terry eyed the feathered scrap on an overhanging ledge and said in whispered disgust, 'But it's grey-black and colourless! How unfair is nature, to give the male birds all the dash and lovely plumage.'

'Nature, I think, does not deal in subtleties.' The Marqués smiled. 'It is the male, after all, who does the wooing, so why should he not be colourful and attractive?'

'Yet how odd it would be,' Terry contested, 'if men in the human species were the more flamboyant of the sexes.'

'In Spain it is often so.' Rafael's dark eyes kindled strangely in the green light. 'The women may glamorise themselves with paint and frills, but in our country the male very definitely does the wooing.'

Terry felt a suffocating need to move on. She displayed a keen interest in a fern-like plant growing nearby and drifted out of Rafael's hold ostensibly to examine it. The move allowed her enough time to regain her composure and from there she idled along as though each new sight was a fresh delight, which in a way it was.

She didn't have to ask if there were more rare species of birds in the locality. Though all were not visible their songs echoed sweetly on the still air. She was beginning to see also now why the valley came to be so named, for carpeting the lower stretches for miles, it seemed, and every available space on the slopes, were the star-leaved, stately lupins. Virgin white every one, their fragile pod-like beauty seemed at variance with the hot blue sky. The perfume too was tantalisingly indistinct but persistent among the dozen and one other scents in the valley.

Noting her smiling preoccupation with the scene, Rafael said, 'The flowers are something of a *fenómeno*. No one knows the story of their origin or the secret of their longevity. Such blooms do not normally survive on the island, preferring cooler skies. As far as is known there is nowhere in this part of the world where they grow in abundance except here in *el valle de los altramuces*.'

Terry took to musing. Had some long-gone relative of Rafael's had connections with England or one of the northern countries? Had some girl-wife, brought back to live on the island, planted a stock of her favourite blooms around the house to remind her of home? It was a foolish fancy, but one Terry didn't want to dispel completely from her mind. Also it gave her something to think about other than Rafael's presence at her side.

She was relieved when they left the overpowering intimacy of the deserted valley and followed a path that climbed gradually until they had reached a rocky platform overlooking the sea. Below were wild beaches unknown to holidaymakers.

Falcons glided here, unaware of their proximity. Rafael told her that the local species were descendants of those brought over by the Moors for falconry sport. There were eagles too, with an incredible wing span, and Terry found it hard to suppress a thrill at their cruel yet majestic predatory flight, somehow fitting, over the windswept terrain.

The green swathe of valley must be a haven, she thought, for all manner of ground life scurrying from those pitiless beaks. As though reading her thoughts the Marqués said, 'Nature protects as well as provides. But in the old days she didn't have it all her own way. Pirate ships often landed here and African corsairs would swarm up the valley and down into the town.'

Terry remarked demurely, 'But an ancestor of yours, I hear, put a stop to all that?'

There was the flash of a white smile. 'Legend, like hearsay, becomes embroidered with time,' he replied with a wry expression. 'It is true a Rafael Quiso led an attack on a pirate lair with devastating results, but unfortunately the raids persisted, though considerably less frequently, up to the end of the sixteenth century.'

Terry was thoughtfully engrossed. So that was how he played down the proud regard of the local fisherfolk. He had neatly sidestepped any claim to fame with his comment, as though from habit. A man with a recognisable force in the vicinity, astute, considerate, and respected, he had no desire to trade on legend, as he called it. Yet seeing him standing here in rough walking attire, his hair unruly, his figure framed against sea and sky, she could almost believe the centuries separating the two Rafael Quisos were mere moments in time.

Of course she kept these kind of fancies to herself, and gazing down towards the furled greenery of the stretch below she mused aloud, 'It's hard to think of anything as awful as villains and cut-throats wrecking the peace of Lupin Valley.'

Rafael nodded. 'It has been this way since Kheir-el-Din's last major raid in Pollensa when eighteen women were taken into slavery.'

'That too?' Terry gave a slight shudder. 'I didn't know. I thought it was just . . . well, plunder.'

'Plunder and slaughter, and the sacking of villages and claiming of women,' he said with ruthless exactness.

Terry asked faintly, 'What would happen to them, those eighteen who were taken so long ago?'

'They would have been subjected to the will of the master of the household.'

She was startled at Rafael's reply. 'But couldn't they have refused, resisted; done something to save themselves from being absorbed into another culture, a violent one at that?' she asked.

His tight mouth curved. 'In North Africa, even today, resistance is a little known word.'

'I don't believe they would have been completely passive,' Terry argued with feeling. 'If I were held against my will in another country I would do something, anything, to maintain my own identity.'

The Marqués' eyes had the ghost of a gleam in them. He said in deep tones, 'You are in a foreign land now. What would you do if you were abducted to some lonely bell-tower retreat?'

Terry met his gaze and looked away. 'The question hardly applies, does it?' she said steadily. 'This is the twentieth century, and we do things with a bit more finesse.'

'If that is what you believe,' Rafael's gleam had become slightly flame-lit, 'then you do not know the true Spain.'

Heart thudding, Terry made some comment to the effect that she ought to be getting back to work. Her emotions were in no way up to coping with this kind of badinage with the Marqués.

They returned by a shorter route and eventually came within sight of the ancient gateway on the ridge slope, marking the entrance to the villa grounds. None of the trek had been taxing, but beside the old gateway structure there was a steep drop of about a hundred feet where the ridge housing the villa came to an abrupt end.

Perhaps because her judgment was clouded with nerves and tension Terry walked too close as they approached the gateway. She would have been in no danger, for the drop sloped gradually from the path. But then her sandal skidded on the dry earth and she had a sensation of lurching towards the void before Rafael's arm came swiftly around her and she was gathered to him on the security and level of the path.

Fright for a moment dulled her senses to what was happening, but soon her mind righted itself to find his body locked close to hers, his eyes but a fraction away from her own gaze. Wildly she asked herself, *Hadn't this happened before somewhere? And wasn't it becoming a habit?* It wasn't just that she would have to watch her step in future when out walking. What was more unsettling was that Rafael always seemed too obligingly close at hand whenever she was about to go sprawling.

The sensible thing now, of course, would have been to move away and brush herself down. Why she didn't was due to a familiar lethargy, a weakness to obey sensible impulses. She could feel his warm breath on her cheek and even while she was recovering from her daze of so much happening so fast, his lips touched hers lightly, briefly.

It all took place in the flurry of the moment and, dreamlike, Terry told herself it must have been her imagination. Either that or Rafael was demonstrating to her just how little twentieth-century 'finesse', as she had called it, could come into lovemaking in Spain.

She had to show that she was level-headed enough to take his little joke in her stride, but how, when the joy of his nearness outshone clear-minded reaction! All she could say when his arms dropped away from her

and they were walking again was a mumbled, 'I've got
so much to do—I really should be getting back to the
villa——'

'Of course. Your all-absorbing work.' A crooked
smile on his lips, his jaw tightening faintly, he led her
to within sight of the house. 'Here is the path to the
rear gardens,' he told her with a slight bow. 'I will
continue on foot to the road.'

Terry didn't know how she got back indoors. Her
legs were almost too weak to hold her, her breath sharp
and painful in her throat. Why did Rafael have to come
here? she asked herself limply. Why did he feel that
she needed tuition in matters of the estate? Of course
to him she was just an assistant, but he was the
Marqués del Alcázar, and with the double game she
was playing with Verna she must never let him see he
had this effect on her.

CHAPTER EIGHT

VERNA arrived back from London annoyed at the time she had had to spend away from Pollensa but pleased with her buying trip. Practically all the name items on the furnishing list had been either purchased or ordered, and those that had eluded her she had engaged scouts in the city to run to ground.

Once back in the cottage she questioned Terry keenly on Rafael's movements. Had he seen much of Miriam Perez?—As though Terry was likely to know the answer to that, though she could guess it with a woman as lovely as the *señorita*—had she, Terry, been putting in a good word for her as she had promised? To this Terry replied, recalling Rafael's protective attitude towards her 'employer', 'It hasn't been necessary. The Marqués has a very high opinion of you.'

'Well, keep polishing my image,' said Verna with a satisfied gleam. 'It all helps towards getting me to the altar.' She tossed her handbag into a chair and unaffected by the silence asked, 'By the way, have you seen Chandler lately?'

'He hasn't been up to the villa, if that's what you mean,' Terry answered flatly.

'No?' Verna's smile was aslant. 'Well, it *has* only been three days. But I was going to say, you see me all right and when I'm the Marquésa I might be able to arrange a little money transaction for you and that layabout Romeo of yours—enough to set you up with a home of your own anywhere off the island.'

Terry made no reply. She had always known that Verna was ninety per cent business-minded and ten per cent woman, and because of this their partnership had prospered. But she had never realised how ruthlessly objective she could be. Not until now, when Rafael de Quiso was the prize.

About a week after Verna's buying trip the goods began to arrive—carpets, plastic-wrapped upholstery, cases of ornamental items, ceramic wall and floor tiles from Madrid, and exotic lighting fitments. Now the villa was no longer deserted. Craftsmen, skilled in the art of fitting a home together, screwed, pasted and hammered, wrecking the peace that Terry had for so long enjoyed. But in a way she didn't mind. It was exciting watching something unfold that had once been no more than an image in her mind, and the gradual birth of design schemes that she had known would be effective filled her with a secret and fearful thrill.

The June heat was enervating and all work at Al Azhar usually came to a stop around noon and was left until the cooler hours after five. For the Majorcans it was a time for dozing and daydreaming in the cool shade, but the holidaymakers and guests at the Hotel Esperanza, caring nothing for *siestas*, splashed in the sea, or soaked up the sun uncomplainingly.

Terry was acquiring something of a tan herself with her afternoon visits to her little private strip of sand around the curve of the beach. Though she was not too far away to be out of view of the hotel terrace she preferred to pretend that it didn't exist when such people as Rafael and Verna and Miriam Perez plus their circle of friends could be seen occupying several chairs on the terrace or frolicking daintly, in Miriam's case at least, in the crystal waters of the terrace beach.

Verna usually contrived to make herself look very attractive in a black bathing suit or eye-catching beach outfit. She had a good figure, if a little on the thin side, and with her thick dark hair and sharpness of expression veiled with a warm smile she was a challenge of sorts to any woman's beauty. Miriam was coquettish and friendly with everyone. She chatted to the men in the party, her inane laughter overlooked, it seemed, or ignored, for she was popular and liked by all. She was certainly not on to any intrigues like the subtle claiming of the Marqués' attention, and because Miriam was sweet and slightly scatterbrained Verna spent many a long session in Rafael's company without the other girl giving it a thought.

And Rafael. Terry worked hard on those afternoons to fight an overpowering awareness of his proximity. She didn't have to look towards the terrace to know that he was there, trim, with the olive-skinned tan of the Spaniard, in swim shorts, or suave in beach slacks and shirt guiding his sport-loving friends along the jetty towards his high-powered ski-boat.

She did, after all, have the diversion of watching the holidaymakers along the strip of sand between her and the terrace, and there were Yves and Pierre, the Frenchmen for companionship.

They were longing to get her to try the windsurfer, and laughing she hedged, 'I'm sure I'd be hopeless at it. I'm not all that confident in deep water—and what would happen if I came off out there in the middle of the bay?'

Yves, the more dashing of the two, drew himself up to his five-foot-something height and with the gallant fervour of the screen hero replied, 'I would get my power dinghy and be there to scoop you in my arms before you could think of feeling afraid!'

You had to hand it to them, they had enough charm to melt the frost off the hardest heart, and Terry's might be going through a traumatic experience, but it was neither hard nor frosty. So it was inevitable that one afternoon she would succumb.

Yves was delighted to play the role of tutor. He assisted her on the float where in a flowered two-piece swimsuit she listened carefully to his instructions. The sail was like a live thing as she levered it into position. Gigantic, or so it seemed, and colourful as befitting Yves's exhibitionist nature, it flapped and wrenched at her arms in the breeze. But it could be manoeuvred or corrected by the metal bow that supported it—or so she was told. The bar, as far as she was concerned, was as slippery and elusive as the fish that darted out of her way in the water. And that went for the float too on which she was expected to find a purchase with her feet while it wobbled at all angles in the waves.

The frequent duckings she took were all in little more than waist-high water, and Yves was always there to tell her where she had gone wrong, while Pierre would go cruising by a few yards away just to demonstrate how easy it was. Unlike him Terry would have many a spectacular fall when the sail would come plummetting down almost on top of her, and gasping and laughing at the hilarity of it, she would come struggling up, game for more of Yves' patient teaching and the inevitable overbalancing into the sea.

But because the Frenchmen were keen to have a pupil who mirrored, if only in an amateurish way, their own fine efforts, she did eventually get the hang of it. With amusement she resigned herself to the fact that she would never win any medals for windsurfing, but at least she could remain upright for fully two or three minutes, and longer if the breeze was not a buffeting one that snatched the sail from her fingers. And Yves and Pierre were pleased, not only because of her small victory, she suspected, but because their combined efforts to make of her a racing queen gave them the status of something more than mere beach acquaintances.

Working at the villa in the cool of the evening was restful after a surfeit of sunshine and often strenuous activity at the beach. There were rooms on the upper floor that still needed some thought, and here Terry would tuck herself away, as far as was possible with the commotion going on below, and gaze abstractedly at the view, which was oddly enough the way she got her best ideas for the interiors.

She didn't see much of Verna at the villa. She was there, of course, with Rafael, supervising the incoming of furniture and fittings with a proprietorial air; giving orders where they were not always necessary to workmen who were dour, but tolerant of her imperiousness. Keen to play the role of the eccentric house designer, she was in danger of over-acting sometimes, but in flame red pants and top or purple bohemian ankle-length slip she always managed to look the part.

Terry avoided the pair as far as possible, but occasionally she was needed to 'assist' Verna with an opinion. One evening the arrival of the white marble figurines which would adorn the archway apertures bordering the main salon terrace caused considerable peturbation.

The weight of each one was colossal and all the possible labour force was mustered on the drive where the consignment had been delivered. On top of this Verna was convinced that some of the statuettes were too large for the apertures. Terry had worked the measurements out carefully. She even knew which pose went into which opening, but to soothe Verna she offered to do a re-check while the other girl made sure the consignment came to no harm during the unloading.

Up on the *salón* terrace Terry didn't need to verify that her calculations were spot-on, but she made a brief check, then waited for the first statuette to appear. It was likely to be a while for no one was sure exactly how transport could be effected.

The evening breeze was still warm, but welcome. It caressed her bare arms and throat and stirred the leafy beginnings of a bougainvillaea being trained around the central archway. The sun was just a golden glow now, lighting up the white houses and buildings of the port and scattering sequin flashes on the millpond waters of the bay.

A footstep sounded on the paved exterior. Terry turned expecting to see a workman with some message perhaps, but it was Rafael who had turned the corner on to the terrace. He came towards her, one dark eyebrow crooking upwards at her leisurely attitude. 'You appear to be content with the aperture's width, *señorita*,' he said, noting the discarded measuring apparatus.

Ever on her guard, Terry replied, 'Verna must have forgotten the accuracy with which she went over these archways ... It's ... understandable, I suppose. She has a lot to think about.'

'Understandable. And of course you had no qualms at all. But your memory is young and lucid, is it not, and you were confident from the start that all was well.'

'That's what I'm here for,' Terry shrugged, not meeting his gaze. 'To smooth the way for Miss Wendell.'

Up here alone with Rafael and the majesty of the scenery she was pulse-jerkingly aware of how long it had been since she had last spoken to him. But not wishing to recall their walk through Lupin Valley, she said stiltedly, 'I thought you were supervising the unloading on the drive.'

'Verna and the foreman have devised a way to transport the marble figurines with a small crane the men use,' he explained. 'It is simply a matter of waiting until all is arranged.'

Stuck for words after that, Terry picked up the steel tape and jotted a few figures on her notepad. She felt Rafael's eyes on her, knew that they detected the sea-water damp of her hair after her beach afternoon. She had put on a sleeveless dress in a soft peach shade which unfortunately enhanced the golden tan of her arms and cheeks. Would he resent, she wondered, her making the most of the island's fabulous weather while she was working for him?

That his mind was centred on much the same subject was obvious when he remarked, 'It surprises me that you have sufficient strength to put in an appearance at Al Azhar after your exertions on the beach.'

'On the contrary, I invariably feel invigorated after a dip,' she replied.

'A dip, or a drowning?' His mouth had that un-pleasant twist to it. He added with this attempt at a smile, 'Windsurfing is too strenuous a sport for a girl.'

'I don't tire easily,' she said lightly.

'True, you are lithe and healthy, but perhaps you do not know that it can also be a little dangerous. The bar supporting the sail is weighty. Without the correct supervision you could be knocked unconscious in the water.'

Terry thought of the charming Yves and Pierre as opposed to Rafael's smouldering disapproval and came back with, 'I have no complaints with my tutors.'

'A pair of ageing French gigolos?'

She flashed him a look. 'Do you always rely on snap judgments for people you've never met?' she asked witheringly. 'I happened to know Yves and Pierre very well and I'd say they have a lot more to recommend them than some of the Spaniards hereabouts.'

'Because of their windsurfing abilities?'

'There's rather more to it than sitting behind the wheel of a luxury speedboat,' she said with a barbed smile.

'And you think that I am not aware of that?' His smile matched hers, but his eyes were lit with a mocking challenge that Terry couldn't quite fathom.

Fortunately the sound of activity drawing nearer gave her the excuse to turn. Seconds later the first of the marble statuettes appeared on a steel trolley, and from then on Terry was kept busy giving directions for the centring and positioning of each one, ostensibly to Verna's satisfaction.

She was glad to have something which kept her fully occupied. She hadn't understood Rafael's odd mood or her own reaction to it, unless one behaved like that when one was in love. Her clash with the Marqués had left her drained, as did any meeting with him. It was a relief when he departed with Verna some time afterwards to attend a cocktail party at the hotel.

When Terry went across to the beach the following afternoon it was with a view to lying and soaking up the sun for a while. Yves and Pierre, being true continentals, did not usually drive along to the sea front until after siesta time about four, so all would be peaceful until then.

She could hear the sound of exuberant holidaymakers as she dozed. But on her little corner of beach they were sufficiently far enough away not to prove a threat to her privacy. She might have drowsed away the whole afternoon, but there was one thing she was learning about the Majorcan sunshine. It was not possible to lie in it for any great length of time, unless one went for an occasional sluicing down in the cool waters.

Reluctant to stir herself but knowing she would get

heat exhaustion if she didn't, Terry paddled in. Once out in the clear depths she was glad she had made the effort. The sea breezes away from the sand tempered the heat and the lethargy fell away from her lapped by refreshing cool wavelets.

She had been swimming and idling perhaps for ten minutes when something making a swishing sound approached at speed. Aware that there were windsurfers in the vicinity Terry made a point of leisurely checking that she was clear. The big crested sail did appear, as she turned, to be on the point of almost running her down. The odd thing was, as she sidestepped it in the water, it came straight on, only ceasing after a deft hand movement displaced the force of the wind and brought the sail to a dead stop no more than a foot from where she floated.

More in admiration than annoyance at the skill of the tight manoeuvre, Terry sought briefly to acknowledge the surfer. It was only in the last moments when something familiar about the lean figure coming into view from behind the sail caught at her heart, then she was gazing into the dark challenging gleam of Rafael.

'*Sube!*' It was an order to get up on the float Terry gathered, not because she understood the command in Spanish, but because there was no mistaking the Marqués' smiling but steely attitude on the matter. She could have swum away, yet something in his manner warned her that this would be a highly dangerous move. If he insisted on giving her a windsurfing lesson it might be wiser, she considered privately, to get it over with.

In her cornflower-blue swimsuit, her skin a lighter gold than his beside her on the float, she had thought he would take to the water, once she had found her footing. Instead he surprised her by grasping the bar of the sail from behind her so that his arms enclosed hers where she gripped it, and his body came close to hers as he positioned his feet, one squarely on each side of hers, on the float.

It had taken him but a moment to affect the stance, after which he flicked the sail so that it bit at the wind and within seconds they were streaking out to sea at breathtaking speed. Terry had never experienced anything so exhilarating in her life. Once she had got over the shock of Rafael's strong arms brushing hers, the hard muscles of his shoulders enclosing her water-damp back, the freedom of the open sea was like wine in her veins.

Out here it was a deep, solid blue whipped into dramatic turbulence by conflicting breezes. The float zipped along guided by Rafael's handling of the bar and with the roar of the wind in their ears, the flapping and tacking of sail, Terry knew breathlessly that she wanted to go on like this for ever, Rafael's body enclosing her own, his tight white smile just a little behind her hair, the thudding of his heart mingling with her own exultant heartbeats.

Speeding at right angles she could see the coastline they were passing; the military zone at the mouth of the bay, with its white villas near the water's edge, housing officials, and golden stone ruins on the hillside of some monastery-like structure which gave it a Grecian aspect. Farther along there were the exclusive blocks of apartments and then the Hotel Esperanza where the guests were small dots lounging on the terrace or swimming beside the sailing jetty. The whole coastline down to the cafes and shops of the town was sprinkled with the emerald green loveliness of pines and tamarisks. The spreading fronds of palms occasionally stirred to show the russet roofs of single and twin-towered villas, and on the edge of the beachside walk the waters surrounding the little pockets of white sand were dappled with the darker greens of sea-grass and moss.

Out here there was none of the security that the beach walk offered. In the middle of the bay, at the mercy of capricious breezes, the loneliness was sometimes awesome and terrifying, yet Terry spurned the security of the world she knew, preferring this wild and tempestuous one where she had never been more alone with Rafael.

Nothing that is blood-tinglingly thrilling can be sustained indefinitely, but long after he had left the rougher seas for the flat waters edging the coastline, her heart continued to pound furiously, and when he came to a stop smoothly on the beach beside the hotel terrace her cheeks gave away her feelings on the adventure.

Rafael made no comment except to toss her a towel from his chair on the terrace. No comment was needed when it came to comparing his handling of a windsurfer with that of Yves and Pierre. And he knew it.

Some of the other members of his group were just returning from a water-skiing excursion, and by the time Terry had patted off the sea-spray and shaken the damp tendrils of her hair from her face she was more or less obliged to stay. Verna, along with one or two other females in the group, had been out in the ski-boat. In harlequin patterned swimsuit, a frill at the hips, she pleaded a thirst, and while Rafael snapped his fingers at a waiter the two young water-skiers who had claimed Terry's attention carried her off for a drink at the open-air bar.

Miriam Perez joined them later. She was at ease in any age group, or rather too frothy-minded to notice if the glances of the younger men were sometimes tolerant, or sometimes laced with secret mirth. Terry liked her tremendously. She might not have had a lot behind those beautiful features, but she bubbled with warmth and animation so that it was impossible not to enjoy her company.

It was through Miriam that Terry found herself a guest at one of the Spanish girl's *tertulias*. It was the birthday of someone in the party, Terry never discovered who, and Miriam had organised a little gathering inside the low-walled, flower-decked area fronting the hotel. Here white tables and chairs were already being arranged by efficient waiters and many of those in the party had gone off to change.

Terry had demurred at first when asked to join in the fun. 'Thanks, Miriam, but I don't think I will,' she had said with a smile. 'I'm really a gatecrasher, you know. My beach bag and dress are where I usually take my swim some way up on the sand.'

'*Nena!* You are Verna's *mano derecha*, are you not?' Miriam had laughingly brushed aside her hesitation. 'So why should you not come along with her to my *tertulia*?'

Hearing herself regarded as Verna's right hand gave Terry a few wry moments inwardly. Her colleague would no doubt be pleased at the term, but she might also consider it 'insubordination' of a kind if she, Terry, attended the gathering.

It was the deep voice that came from behind then that had left her no alternative. '*Claro!* What Miriam says is true. Where would we be without the efficiency of our assistant at Al Azhar? And assistants must sometimes show themselves, if only at an afternoon tea-party. *No es así?*'

She had turned to meet Rafael's hard mocking expression and knew that it had not pleased him to hear Miriam's invitation being rejected. Or perhaps he was letting her know that as *el dueño*, or her employer, in the true sense of the word, his girl-friend's wishes should be obeyed without question. The windsurfing incident was still powerful in both their minds, as her blue glance locked briefly with his forceful dark one, then she was saying politely, 'Very well. I'll go and tidy up.'

There was no sign of Verna as she skirted the terrace to collect her things, which made it fairly certain that her partner was changing in the privacy of Rafael's apartment.

Terry herself didn't intend to go to great lengths with her appearance and found the powder room of the hotel adequate for her needs. Her hair still curled damply with sea-spray and there were other telltale lingerings of her recent adventures in the eyes that stared back at her from the mirror, but her sundress, patterned with pink and white magnolias, did just about rise to the occasion, she discovered later as she mingled with similarly dressed female members of the party.

Verna, of course, was slightly exotic in flowered chiffon trousers and bolero over tangerine knitted cotton. It was odd how her hard features, nut-brown now with the sun, could appear strikingly attractive in a setting such as this. Miriam Perez, her usual vague and rapt-minded self, was, in contrast, almost starkly simple in sleeveless white silk. The men wore summer slacks and shirt, with a tie of course in deference to Miriam. Terry wondered if Rafael had been instrumental in setting the fashion. In pearl-grey sports trousers and shirt and light silk tie he looked the epitome of Spanish courtesy and charm.

Of course she never let her glance stray more than once or twice in his direction, and then mainly to note that Verna was becoming adept at bringing a smile to his lips. Instead Terry sought to ease the turmoil that was going on inside her after her wordless clash with the Marqués on the waves, in the company of less disturbing men. There were plenty of these on hand. Most of those enjoying the hospitality of the hotel were Rafael's business friends. Steve Arnold was the British representative of a Quiso wine firm. Only in Majorca for a few days he was making the most of the amenities available. He had commandeered Terry's company by piling her plate high with food from the buffet tables and plying her with stories of his adventures in the wine trade.

Terry was in no mood for eating. Much of Miriam's choice for the party was far too rich for her taste in any case: moist almond pastry shapes, pale cake oozing thick white cream, apple squares glistening with honey topping. Even the dainty rolls bulging with succulent fillings were of the sweet kind! What odd tastes Spanish ladies had.

But at least it was an animated gathering and she could pretend with some effort that what had happened some time earlier on the water had affected her in no way at all. She was listening to a rather exciting account of Steve Arnold's brush with army personnel at a South American Customs post when a commotion near at hand caused most of those in the gathering to turn.

'Mamá!' 'It was Miriam's cry that rent the party atmosphere and all eyes followed her delighted flight to where an official-looking car had stopped outside the low-walled surround fronting the hotel entrance.

The woman who alighted with the assistance of a uniformed chauffeur was Miriam's double. The same sylph-like figure, jet hair and beautiful features which, though grown slack with age, marred none of the exquisite bone structure. She could have passed for an older sister, but there was one distinct difference in the family resemblance. The stony, shrewd light in the mother's eyes was far removed from the gay, abstracted look in those of the daughter.

The two embraced effusively and rattled away in Spanish for a while, then Miriam, conscious of her duties as a hostess, switched to the international language for the benefit of her guests. '*Madre mia!* What a darling surprise! But why didn't you tell us you were flying out from Madrid? Did you want to catch us at some naughty game? Wicked Mamá, coming to spy on us. But I do love you! How is Papá? Did you tell him I lost my emerald bracelet on Gunther's speedboat? Poor Papá! Was he very angry . . .?'

Once the arrival had been acknowledged and the guests saw that the conversation continued to be of a personal nature they returned to their own amusements. Terry too would have preferred to remain anonymous listening to Steve Arnold's chat, but to her horror she heard herself being singled out as Miriam prattled on, 'Mamá, you must meet our sweet little Teresa. She works long hours following orders at Rafael's villa and we hardly ever see her poor child. *Por cierto*, she would not have come to my party this afternoon if Rafael hadn't insisted . . .'

The Marqués had been the first to greet Señora Otero-Perez with a low bow and the brush of his lips against the back of her hand. Now the woman cast a swift, but all-embracing, glance over Terry, who had been obliged to come forward, and cutting across her daughter's vapid chat she asked flintily, 'And who is that lady over there?'

'*Ay que tonteria!* How silly of me! Verna, come here and meet Mamá. Madre, this is the clever interior designer whom everyone is talking about, and little Teresa's boss, of course. They say she is doing wonders with the rooms at Rafael's villa . . .'

Verna smiled, completely at ease, and spoke quietly in contrast to Miriam's harsh patter. 'Good afternoon, *señora.* I hope you had a pleasant flight from the capital?'

With a touch of asperity the woman replied, 'These journeys have to be made, madam. Even in Spain we are learning to take advantage of speedy air travel.'

Terry was recalling the gossipy Señora Carra's chat that first evening in Rafael's hotel suite. According to her Miriam's mother was dead set on having the Marqués as a son-in-law, and judging by her frigid reception of Verna just now her eagle eye had spotted the two of them in close companionship on her arrival. Or perhaps it was rumours of such an alliance circulating as far as Madrid which had brought her here. Either way, Verna had never been known to let a snub pierce her equable front, and smoothly she went on making light conversation while Miriam, no match for her calculating experience, joined in all unsuspectingly.

Terry would have liked to disappear back among the guests, but Señora Perez asked her what her assistant duties consisted of at the villa. Her insides constricted as she hoped her replies sounded casual enough.

It was the Marqués who saved her from a prolonged encounter with the rather formidable woman by suggesting she take some refreshment after her journey. 'I want a bath after travelling across the island in your damnable humidity,' the Señora said without preamble. 'Give me the dryness of Madrid any day. I hope, Rafael,' she fixed him with her pebbly gleam, 'you have an air-conditioned suite at my disposal?'

'But of course, Rosa,' he offered her his arm. 'There is always the best on hand for the *gran dama* of our two families.'

He led her indoors and the partygoers soon forgot the interruption in the business of enjoying themselves. All except Terry. With the arrival of Miriam's mother she was gripped by a fresh feeling of apprehension, a conviction that life for her on the island and at Rafael's villa was going to be even more precarious than it had been in the past.

The one thing that eased the strain of playing a false role for Terry was her walks in Lupin Valley. Verna invariably lunched with Rafael at the hotel, and rather than eat alone at the cottage Terry often packed a picnic lunch, and when the morning's work was done at Al Azhar she would follow one of the paths into the soothing greenery and peace of another world.

Here there were no worries about fathoming Rafael's rather penetrating glances, no cause for tight nerves wondering if she had let some hint of the truth slip out in innocent conversation. Here she had only the colourful birds for company, the rustle of the breeze among the swaying lupins, and the distant murmur of the sea, heightened because of the silence of the valley.

Butterflies of brilliant blue, cream, and purple would pause to show off their wings in some spot in the sunshine and all manner of insects created a symphony of sound in the undergrowth where great yellow and black striped spiders would wait at the key point of an elaborately woven web for food for their larder.

Terry could always find something to take her mind off her own feeling of desolation, and even when she returned to the villa there was the secret thrill of seeing her ideas taking shape. She was torn between being pleased or wincing that they were turning out better than even she had envisaged.

As most of the groundwork had been done in the initial designing she was supposed to be merely supervising the actual putting together of these plans. But she loved being on hand watching the craftsmen bring to life the visions she had first had in her mind.

Of course, Verna's presence in the capacity of designer was rarely needed now, but this too suited Terry. On her own at Al Azhar she could ache at the thought of Verna and Rafael being alone somewhere. But at least she didn't have to go through the stress of being near to him and at the same time deceiving him.

If Miriam's mother was a force in Madrid she didn't appear to have much say here, but that could be because Rafael, though courteous and respectful, intended to suit himself where marriage was concerned. And if his choice for a wife was Verna he was the kind of person who would go ahead with his own plans while keeping the peace in his own suave way with those who opposed him. But being a man he couldn't know the wiles that a woman with Rosa Perez' motives could get up to to obtain her desires, and for her money, Terry mused wryly, she wouldn't care to cross the Spanish matriarch at any time.

The shopping still had to be done for the cottage, if only mainly for herself these days. She had seen Leigh at the Bar Fabula once or twice on her trips to town, but on the last two or three buying expeditions there had been no sign of him. She knew that his birdwatching schemes had so far come to nothing, and while being a little impatient of his failure to take up opportunities when they were offered him, it worried her to think of him drifting with no fixed ideas for supporting himself. Then one day he turned up in Lupin Valley, of all places, taking her completely by surprise.

Terry often wandered out to the sea opening to watch the wild majesty of the eagles and the rather fearsome sight of black vultures over this forsaken stretch of coast. In the noonday heat it was pleasant to dip her feet in rougher waters than those that caressed the tourist beaches around the headland. She had redone her sandals on this occasion and strolled up the

slope that brought her to the mossy crest where she
had stood with Rafael that morning.

She never came to this spot without recalling those
heart-stopping moments beside him, when his hair had
lifted in the wind and his teeth had shone as strong
and as white as those in the smiles of the swashbuckling
types they had been discussing at the time. Indeed,
her heart leapt now as she heard a sound close by.
Idiotically thinking it was him, she turned, but the
person who emerged from the screening bushes bore
no resemblance to the proud, lean figure of Rafael de
Quiso.

Leigh was dressed in what had once been a pair of
jeans, but which, now chopped off at the thighs, were
enjoying a second lease of life as frayed shorts, plus a
tee-shirt whose trendy message had worn into un-
readability with age. The heat had no doubt made this
kind of outfit necessary, but it did nothing to enhance
Leigh's unshaven, lank-haired appearance. Even so
Terry was touched by a look of vulnerability about his
youthful features, and brushing aside an uneasy feeling
at his weird choice of meeting place she ran forward,
pleasure in her voice. 'Leigh! Where have you been
hiding yourself? I've been to the Bar Fabula several
times lately without seeing a sign of you.'

'I've been around,' he smiled noncommittally,
adding as he dropped down to sprawl full length on
the grass, 'Studying form, you might say . . . you know,
the local scene and what it has to offer.'

'And have you come up with anything?' Terry asked
hopefully, lowering herself into a sitting position
beside him.

He shrugged, reaching for a piece of grass to chew,
'Depends.' While Terry was wondering what he meant
by this he turned to look at her and with the green
stem between his teeth, he said, 'That time up at the

villa, I got to thinking that property was a pretty good thing to be in on. Got to know a couple of estate agents along this stretch of coast. Might be on to something, but as I say, it depends.'

'On what?' Terry asked, intrigued.

'You'll see.' Leigh clasped his hands under his head and staring at the sky he asked, 'How's the work going with the big chief in these parts?'

'I don't see much of the Marqués,' Terry answered levelly. 'The house is coming along, though. Some of the main rooms are almost completed.'

'Fancy villas are cropping up along the coast from here down to Santanyi on the south-eastern tip,' said Leigh, giving only half an ear to her reply. 'The types who are having them built are moneyed all right, but they don't come in to your Marqués' class.' As Terry made no comment he explained with a grin, 'What I mean is they don't go in for smart interior decorators like your boss, the Wendell dame. Naturally they like to be up on all the latest gimmicks, but as their millions don't run into being one hundred per cent exclusive they usually make do with what they can work out for themselves interior-wise, and any ideas that are going.'

Terry nodded, though she didn't find the conversation terribly gripping. She would far rather have heard Leigh telling her that he had truly been making an effort to find a good paying job for himself. Or at least that he had been considering accepting the Marqués' offer of employment in Marbella. Despair made her smile a little sadly as she eyed him where he lay spread-eagled on the grass, the stem between his teeth twirling as he toyed with his thoughts.

She had almost forgotten what they had been talking about when he suddenly propped himself up on one elbow and said, 'Tell me about the work you do at the Quiso villa.'

'Oh, a hundred and one things!' she hedged smilingly.

'Yeah, I suppose so.' Was there impatience in his grin? 'But you must be in on the finished result somewhere. For instance,' he appeared to pause for inspiration, 'the room that faces the mountains and looks out on to the patio where we met that day. How's it doing?'

'The smaller *salón*?' Terry considered. 'It's almost finished, we're just waiting for one or two items.'

'So tell me about it. Is the Marqués going to rave, do you think? I mean, what does it look like?'

At this rather avid interest Terry took to musing aloud. 'Well, it's green and white and cool-looking, and its main charm I think is——' She stopped herself abruptly and looked at Leigh. 'But I shouldn't be giving . . . Miss Wendell's secrets away.' A cold prickle ran along her skin. She had almost forgotten herself then.

'Aw, come off it! I thought you and I were pals!' The scorn in Leigh's voice was made more noticeable by something like impatience, though his grin remained as he added in injured tones, 'The first time I take an interest in what you do for a living and you come at me with a top-secret attitude!'

'It's nice to talk to you, Leigh,' Terry said with a grave smile, 'but we both know I shouldn't be divulging the layout and contents of the Villa Al Azhar's interiors without permission.'

'Okay, okay! Forget it.' Leigh sat up, hugged his knees and frowned morosely at the sea.

Terry was hurt at his mood, but trying not to show it she pleaded gently, 'Can't we talk about anything except the villa?'

'I thought I was doing you a favour,' he flung at her. 'What else can we talk about? For sure not what I do to make a greasy dollar.'

There was a miserable silence, then as though to disperse it Leigh said, 'Look. I was simply curious to know what it was like being assistant to a sought-after house designer. If you don't want to discuss trade secrets, okay. But what about the rest of the villa, the places that haven't been titivated yet? Are we safe there?'

Terry wasn't quite sure what he meant, but she nodded. 'There are still some of the smaller apartments on the upper floors to be attended to. The Marqués' dressing room, for instance.'

'You're sure it's all right to talk about an empty room?'

The bitter sarcasm cut deeply, but Terry reminded herself that Leigh had had a rough time of it lately. Compassion outweighing all other emotion, she offered, 'If you'd really like to hear I could tell you some of the ideas that . . . Miss Wendell has in mind for this particular section.'

The young man's bad humour seemed to dissolve. He leaned close and putting his arm round her he said with his old grin, 'I don't want to fight with you, Terry. Haven't you guessed I like to know how you spend your time?'

'Oh, I'm glad we're friends again,' Terry laughed with feeling. 'It was awful, biting each other's heads off like that.' Though she didn't recall that she had done much biting. 'I'm always thinking about you, Leigh,' she went on while she gazed searchingly into his face. 'How you're managing out here in a foreign country, now that your father's——'

'Yeah—well, don't worry about me. I'll survive. You were saying . . . about the Marqués' pad.'

It was some moments before Terry could reshuffle her thoughts, but now that Leigh had regained his good mood she had no wish to upset him again. She pondered awhile, then spoke her ideas aloud, being careful, of course, to mask their true source. 'Well, the walls are to be in quilted leather, I think, because in Miss Wendell's opinion this gives a truly masculine aura . . . and I agree with her. Red is her choice, with black leather border at ceiling level. The quilting will be picked out with gold studs and will also decorate some of the furnishing in the room; the valet side-table, the accessories bureau, the cocktail cabinet . . . We'll have two armchairs in black leather and the floor will be in veined marble vinyl. . . .'

Carried away now, for she knew by heart what she had planned for Rafael's dressing room, Terry went on to describe everything in detail, though it was all still a dream in her mind. And, lost to her surroundings while picturing the effect, she paid little attention to Leigh's queries here and there except to verify them. 'Did you say a black leather border round the ceiling?'—'Was it sailing scenes you mentioned for the frosted glass fronting the shirt cabinets?'

When she had finished she felt reasonably proud that she had slanted all responsibility for design neatly Verna's way, but Leigh appeared to lose interest. After sitting quite still through her description he said with an offhand grin, 'So that's what goes on in the day of a decorator's assistant,' then searched around for another subject.

Terry smiled ironically to herself. It was a good job Leigh wasn't her only critic, however unknowing. She asked in good humour, 'And what goes on in the day of a former birdwatching guide?'

'Oh . . . things—and that reminds me,' he stood up, 'I'll have to be going. It's been great talking to you, Terry, but you know how it is—*tempus fugit*.'

A little bemused, she waved him off and watched

him disappear quickly along the beach and round the headland. Well, she would have to watch she didn't become a bore when it came to talking shop!

The heat was increasing and Terry found her trips to the beach as much a necessity as a way of escaping from her problems at the villa. The sea was the only place to keep cool pleasantly and she had company here of the kind that made no demands on her emotions. But one afternoon she was devastated to learn that it was Yves' and Pierre's last day on the island.

For a whole month she had joked and splashed with them until now it seemed that they had become a fixture in her life at the beach. It wouldn't be the same without them. The dashing Frenchmen were popular with the tourists and well known for their sporting activities on the water. The news that they would be driving to the ferry at Alcudia tonight en route for France filled Terry with a feeling of desolation. But then holiday friendships were destined to be tinged with sadness, she told herself, watching them take their windsurfers out for the last time.

She hadn't been back at the cottage long that afternoon when something happened which drove all thoughts of the departure of her favourite beach companions from her mind. The Marqués' official car drew up outside and the uniformed figure of the chauffeur Fernando came along the path to where she was watering her potted cuttings in the shade. He handed her a sealed envelope and said, 'Doña Rosa Otero-Perez has asked me to give you this.'

Rosa Perez sending written messages to her? Terry opened the letter, her fingers stiff with apprehension. The writing was on the Marqués' official paper and the tone was polite but imperious.

Señorita Heatherton,

I wish to speak with you alone. It would please me if you could present yourself at my suite at the Hotel Esperanza at nine-thirty tonight, where we can sit undisturbed with a cocktail aperitif. Fernando will collect you at the appointed hour and drive you to the hotel.

Rosa Otero-Perez

Terry's fingers holding the letter went icy cold. What did Miriam's mother want with her? She was simply an 'assistant' at the Villa Al Azhar, wasn't she, with little connection with the Marqués' set. But it was clear there could be no ignoring the message, which was framed like an invitation and read like a command. And the chauffeur had orders to *collect* her in any case.

Aware that Doña Rosa Otero-Perez was a woman accustomed to being obeyed, Terry was nevertheless moved to one small act of defiance as she told the chauffeur, 'There's no need to call and pick me up tonight, Fernando. It's only ten minutes' walk and I know my way.'

'But the Señora stressed . . .'

At his doubtful look she gave him a reassuring smile. 'It's all right, I'll be there.'

With this he returned down the path and drove away, and Terry was left with a hollow feeling in the pit of her stomach. She recalled all too well her first and only meeting with Rosa Perez when she had first arrived at the hotel from Madrid. Terry had sensed that she was a woman of keen insight then, and with all she had to hide the Señora was the last person she would choose to share in a pleasant *tête-à-tête*. But more than this she had a feeling that tonight's meeting was to do with Verna.

The cooling blue glow of dusk was softening the villa estate as she left the cottage and started out for the hotel. She had put on a cream-coloured dress whose plainness was offset by a spangled thread running through the weave, for her interview with Miriam's mother. The high crags overlooking this stretch of coast appeared brooding beneath their sable mantle of night. Or was it just Terry's nerves, knowing that the next half hour or so was not going to be easy? Certainly the other villas, aloof, exclusive and silent, offered her no encouragement.

She was just about to cross the Formentor road when the low purr of a car coming from behind her along the avenue of the villa estate made her stop to allow it to turn out. Her heart lifted a rung when she recognised it as Yves and Pierre's golden estate car. What a happy coincidence! If she had been waiting to wave them off she couldn't have timed it better. Luggage aboard, their windsurfers strapped to the roof, they were obviously just starting out for the night ferry round the bay at Alcudia.

The Frenchmen too were delighted at this unexpected opportunity of bidding her a nocturnal farewell. '*Ah, mon Dieu, ma chérie!* We have to leave your beautiful isle. But next year we will meet again, *non?*'

Terry just smiled and nodded and wished them *bon voyage*. Once her work at the villa was finished, and pray to heaven it wouldn't be too long now, nothing would bring her to this part of the world again.

But at the moment she was genuinely pleased to be able to wish her gallant beach companions a last goodbye. She chatted with them for a few moments, discovering that it would take them thirty-six hours to make the journey through the Mediterranean and across France to their home town of Arromanches. Yves, the shorter and plumper of the two, was looking tanned and boldly attractive in a pale linen safari suit. Pierre, always more conventional, sat upright and smiling in blue blazer and slacks.

Giving them a last wave, Terry knew that she was going to miss them both a great deal. There was even the suggestion of a tear in her eye as she watched the estate car pull slowly away and disappear in the gloom along the road. It was only when its rear lights had ceased to be visible that she became aware of another car quite close at hand. Stationary, with a figure just alighting, it must have drawn up some moments ago, but she had been too occupied to notice it.

She was blazingly aware of it now, of course, for there was no mistaking its pale opulence, or the bearing of the man who approached her in the shadows.

'Very touching,' Rafael said in harsh tones. 'You have all the tragedy of the deserted half of a holiday affair in your wave.'

Terry turned her over-bright gaze away from him and said tersely, 'I don't think affection is anything to be ashamed of, *señor*. And I don't mind admitting I'm sorry to see my friends leaving.'

'You will need to harden yourself against such departures, *señorita*.' Rafael was coldly sarcastic. 'You do not possess the robust disposition to cope with it all summer.'

'I shall always be sad to see an acquaintance of mine leave the island.' Terry raised her chin at him. 'You may be used to it, owning a hotel, but I could never be indifferent to the going out of my life of someone whose company I have enjoyed.'

'By that you mean you will pine inwardly like an abandoned puppy on every occasion. But of course you are too young to know that this kind of hurt has, one day, got to be mastered.' For a moment the impatience dropped from his manner, and his smile was taut and white as he asked, 'I too will soon have to leave the island on matters of business. Will you miss me?'

Terry looked at him briefly and then away again, her heart choking her in her throat. Miss him! She missed him all the hours of the day and night he was out of her sight. And to think of him in some other part of the hemisphere filled her with an altogether different kind of desolation. But as he had said, one had to learn to live with this sort of despair.

Choosing her words carefully, she murmured, 'That's different, *señor* . . . I hardly know you . . .' She was thinking with heat under her cheeks of that moment on the ridge path above Lupin Valley, when he had saved her from slithering towards the incline. But any man would have done that, she reminded herself soberly. And the sensation, when he had caught her close to him, that his lips had brushed against hers could only have been her imagination. Or to be more exact, the position she was in at the villa would not permit her to believe otherwise.

'True, I am simply *el dueño*, the Spanish master whose house you are preparing, am I not?' His smile straightened into an austere line. He took her arm and guiding her to his car, explained, 'You rejected the assistance of my chauffeur, so I myself have come to accompany you to Doña Rosa Perez's apartment.'

'It's ridiculous to suggest that I need transport, or an escort!' Baulking at being propelled along in this way, Terry stopped short at the open doorway. 'It's no more than a few minutes' walk to the hotel, and I like to take the evening air.'

'*Desde luego*. And there are other pleasures to be derived from strolling in the twilight, as we have seen.' With a sneering reference to the Frenchmen's departure he installed her in the car with a firm hand, adding as he came to sit behind the driving wheel, 'But while

you are in a way my responsibility, Miss Heatherton,
permit me to maintain the old-fashioned belief that a
young woman should not be abroad in the evening
hours unescorted.'

The atmosphere in the interior for the short drive
was decidedly tense. Rafael didn't know that she had
purposely sought a few moments alone to brace herself
for her session with Rosa Perez. Also there was an
annoyed glitter in his eyes that seemed to go deeper
than her mere refusal to accept the services of his
chauffeur.

CHAPTER NINE

TERRY moved from Rafael as soon as they entered the Hotel Esperanza, thanking him woodenly for his consideration and making straight for the lift. She had no burning desire to meet Miriam's mother, but even less did she feel like lingering in Rafael's company under the circumstances. He pressed the appropriate button for her and watched her depart upwards with a slight bow.

It was a good thing, she counted her blessings in trembling state on the ascent, that the Marqués hadn't seen fit to issue them with rooms at the hotel for their stay on the island. That, to Terry's mind, would have made the situation impossible.

Señora Perez herself answered the doorbell. That she would have been supplied with a maid at Rafael's orders for her stay at the Esperanza was a foregone conclusion, but tonight she appeared to have got rid of room staff for Terry's visit.

'*Bueno*, Miss Heatherton, you are on time! If only we Spaniards could learn to be so punctual.' She waved Terry in and latched the door carefully behind her while keeping up a flow of hard, bright chat. 'When I'm on the island I altogether despair. No one seems to know what a clock looks like, let alone own one! A fixed appointment can mean any time from noon onwards, and I avoid wherever possible making business dates. I value my blood pressure too much. Of course, in Madrid city habits have all but dispensed with the *mañana* attitude, but even there I must confess to a certain *laéssez-faire*. It's disgraceful but we are a lethargic race and *por supuesto*, we will never alter.'

By this time Terry had been shown to a winged armchair, of which there were two almost facing each other. A small table set with silver tray and drinks had been placed at the side. 'You will take a little refreshment, Miss Heatherton?' The piercing dark eyes were trained on her as the older woman sat down opposite her.

'No, thank you, Doña Rosa,' Terry refrained politely. 'You said you wished to speak to me, but I'm wondering if there's been some mistake. We've met only once on your arrival, and I'm ... simply an employee at the Villa Al Azhar.'

'No, there has been no mistake.' Those lovely, but ageing lips, pursed into a businesslike smile. 'And like you I have no desire to waste time on preamble, so we shall get straight to the point. My request to speak with you concerns your associate at the villa, Miss Verna Wendell.'

Terry felt a chill creeping along her veins. 'I'm not sure I understand you, *señora*,' she said, her gaze unwavering.

'Speaking in all frankness, *señorita*,' Rosa Perez' attitude tightened imperceptibly, 'I wish to know something of your employer's background. Perhaps you are not aware that the Marqués spends a great deal of time with her, and the woman's possessive airs are becoming the talk of the community.'

'Surely that is something that concerns only the two of them?' Terry said levelly.

The Spanish woman permitted herself a curled smile. 'Rafael believes I have asked you here tonight because of a maternal concern for his Cinderella assistant. He would not condone any kind of subterfuge behind his back, but you and I, *señorita*——'

'Count me out, *señora*.' Terry was firm but polite.

'Local gossip is not my concern. If there's something you want to know about Miss Wendell why not ask her yourself?' She had hoped by her negative attitude to discourage further probing, but far from being put off the scent Rosa Perez spoke her thoughts aloud with narrowed gaze.

'She is clever, that woman. Clever, talented and successful. And yet there is a loose fitting somewhere— how would you say?—a bad connection in her make-up. What I am trying to say, *señorita*, is that Miss Wendell is not all confidence. Sometimes I sense a lack of it in her manner. It is fleeting, I admit, comes and goes like the whiff of jasmine in a garden, but it is there, a secret worry perhaps, a recurring uncertainty.'

'If you will pardon my mentioning it, Doña Rosa,' while stiffening inwardly Terry said with the semblance of a smile, 'it was probably nothing more than your rather forthright regard which unsettled her at the time.'

'You think so?' Rosa Perez was unconvinced. She went on speaking her thoughts. 'It is not that I would not wish to admit that Miss Wendell has all the attributes to make Rafael a good wife. . . .'

'But your daughter Miriam would make him a better one?' Still bold, Terry was ready to try anything to get the conversation on to a less dangerous level.

Señora Perez' smile was not just one of affection, it revealed a naked motherly love that was almost unnerving to behold. 'Miriam is the sole fruit of my marriage with Don Sebastian Perez.' The words were spoken proudly. 'She may not be all that a mother could wish for in a daughter—It is for this reason that I will know no peace until her life is made secure. She will marry Rafael de Quiso.'

This ultimatum gave Terry her cue, and making to rise she murmured, 'As I have pointed out, *señora*, none of this concerns me. And now, if you'll excuse me——'

'Your loyalty towards your employer is understandable, Miss Heatherton.' The Spanish woman ignored Terry's efforts to extricate herself from the interview and pursued indomitably '. . . And yet I wonder at it. You do not mind her reaping the acclaim while you do the hard work behind the scenes?'

'Effort is a relative thing.' While appearing to sound offhand Terry was acutely aware of Rosa Perez' piercing gaze on her, ray-like it seemed, and lighting up all the hidden corners of her mind.

'How long have you worked for Miss Wendell?' was the net result of that look.

'About a year,' Terry answered cautiously.

'And what did she do before that?'

'As I don't know I can't tell you.' It was a relief to be able to answer truthfully, though this was short-lived.

'But she wasn't a successful interior designer then,' Rosa Perez divined shrewdly.

Deeming it wiser to remain silent, Terry was conscious of that searchlight gaze still probing her mind, and rising abruptly she paved the way for her departure with a smile which, try as she might, was inclined to be tremulous. 'I'm afraid I must go now. Thank you for inviting me——'

Señora Perez rose too, almost languidly, and waved a hand to slow down Terry's flight. 'We are dining in Rafael's suite tonight. It was his idea that you should come along too.' And, her regard as keen and relentless as ever, Rosa added pleasantly, 'We shall discover another time, perhaps, what it is you are hiding concerning Miss Wendell.'

Terry didn't know which was worst, having to remain

under Rosa's covert scrutiny, or being in the same room as Rafael for the rest of the evening. Without the other guests she would have been in emotional shreds, but fortunately Miriam was there among half a dozen others, so there was no danger of the conversation becoming heavy.

Mother and daughter would surely be the star attraction at any gathering, Terry thought. Miriam had inherited her mother's fragile beauty; that alabaster smoothness of features and proud turn of the head. But as far as Terry was concerned there the similarities ended. After her session with Rosa Perez, she was inclined to liken her to a predatory tigress, whereas Miriam was a gambolling lamb.

She did almost gambol among the other guests, laughing and chattering at top speed. She had taken a liking to Terry—not that she didn't love everyone— and unfortunately singled her out with an arm about her shoulder, at one point, to call across the room, 'Raffy *querido*, why don't we take our little English friend on the tour we once talked about? And Verna too. Poor *chicas*! You are a wicked, wicked *dueño* to work them so.'

'I'm really very busy at the moment,' Terry said hurriedly.

Rafael rested his gaze on her and with a slight tightening of his smile he replied, 'You are right, Miriam. A holiday from the tasks at the villa is long overdue. I myself came to this conclusion a day or so ago, and have taken the liberty of organising a trip in two cars which will cover a few of the tourist attractions, and certainly the lesser-known beauty spots on the island. We will go on the *fiesta* of next week, and as well as the whole of Spain our two charming house beautifiers will take a day off too.'

While Terry's heart twisted in her breast Miriam

exclaimed laughingly, '*Estupendo! Fantastico!* You and I and Teresa and Verna will go in the lead car. And Mamá can come too if she wishes.'

Señora Perez made no direct comment as to what she would do on the day. Verna too only smiled from where she was draped on the arm of a chair, looking tanned and glamorous in a case-hardened way. She never openly pushed her claim for Rafael when Miriam's mother was around. If Rosa was a watchful tigress protecting her young, Verna was a sleek cat of another breed, one that is content to bide its time in its quest for the prey.

In the cottage later that evening she looked pleased with the outcome of the dinner party. 'I thought Rafael would never ask us!' She gave a dry laugh, tossing aside a gold weave cape. 'I must say I'm getting sick of seeing what passes for a town round here. It will be interesting to discover what the rest of the island has to offer. If it's as dead-and-alive as this place, I only hope Rafael will spend most of the year in Madrid after we're married.'

Terry suspected that Verna, when not at the villa, was left to spend long periods with little diversion. Rafael was not a man to neglect business commitments and it sounded as though she found little to amuse herself when he was not around.

Before they went to their separate bedrooms Terry said, 'Verna, do you think it would matter greatly if I didn't go on the trip?'

The other girl gave her a sharp look. 'I thought you'd be glad to get out of this backwater, if only for a day?'

Terry shrugged. 'Surprisingly I like it here. And I could spend the day finishing those sketches for the villa entrance and side dining terrace.' She could feel Verna's gaze raking her, noticing no doubt her shadowed eyes and pale face. No matter, she couldn't face a whole day in Rafael's company. She had made up her mind tonight to get the villa finished as quickly as possible and get away from here. Leave the island and Verna and go somewhere where she could forget this disastrous episode in her life. Disastrous and painful, for there was the thought that she would never see Rafael again. But what was the sense in prolonging the agony? Love was based on an honest relationship, one that she had never had or could ever hope to have with the Marqués del Alcázar. And anyway, there were Miriam and Verna. If Verna turned out to be the winner in the battle for Rafael's hand she would have to run the gauntlet of Rosa's monumental displeasure, and that would not be an enviable task.

She wasn't prepared for Verna's comment when it came, which showed she believed mistakenly that Terry's lacklustre appearance was due to another cause. 'Still wondering about that layabout Leigh Chandler?' she queried. 'You're a fool to worry about someone who could be a drag on you for the rest of your life. But that's your business, I suppose.' About to drop the subject, she asked, 'By the way, where is he keeping himself these days? Not permanently stuck at the villa, is he? It's like him to find himself a cushy spot for his stay on the island, and you're fool enough to be a party to smuggling him into some lush furnished room for the night.'

Terry's insides went cold at the words. She never ceased to wonder at the noxious intricacies of Verna's mind, nor at the depths she would stoop to show her contempt for the weak-minded.

'I haven't seen him for some time,' she said quietly, though not without spirit. 'But I hope he's managing all right at whatever he's trying to do to earn money.'

Already bored with the subject, Verna waved a hand.

'Well anyway, about the car drive. You needn't come
if you don't want to. That will leave just the two of us
with the Marqués, and I can handle Miriam.' On her
way to bed she added, 'And I think it's a good idea to
speed up the finishing touches at the villa. Rafael is
obviously not going to make a move until the house is
ready for his bride, and quite frankly I've had enough
of that battleaxe would-be mother-in-law of his. She's
too nosy for her own good, and besides, she gives me
the creeps.'

During the next few days Terry worked harder than
she had ever worked at Al Azhar, following up the
workmen at their duties, supervising the hanging of
curtains though the seamstresses could have managed
quite well without her. But every job completed, she
felt, was a moment nearer her escape. Every minute
prolonged was coupled with the risk of someone discovering the truth about the Wendell-Heatherton
association, and if and when they did she wanted to be
miles away from Rafael's accusing gaze.

But there were other times when she knew a dreadful
ache at having to leave. Occasions when she wandered
alone in Lupin Valley and listened to the sweet singing
of the hidden feathered life. But even here she couldn't
escape the feeling of desolation, for the flowers, those
proud white spears of virgin beauty, were shrivelling
fast in the July heat and all that remained on the slopes
and valley floor were yellowing stems. They would
return in the spring, but that was an eternity away, as
was the comparatively carefree existence that Terry
had enjoyed on her arrival on the island.

The day of the car tour came, and Verna suggested
that they should plead a sprained ankle where Terry
was concerned. She saw no reason to argue with this
and remained indoors for the morning as a safeguard.

Verna didn't arrive back until almost midnight, when
Terry was in bed, but judging by her satisfied air the
next morning the outing had gone according to her
wishes.

Terry had finished all the sketches. This pleased
Verna too, though she didn't offer to accompany her
to the villa to see how results were shaping up. She
did, however, give Terry a lift to the gateway entrance,
apologising offhandedly for needing the hired car for a
trip to town.

Terry spent the whole day in the vicinity of the villa.
The long walk up from and down to the road was not
one anyone would wish to attempt more than once in a
day and fortunately she had brought a picnic lunch
with her. She ate it at one of her favourite spots in
Lupin Valley, then returned to put in more work at Al
Azhar.

It was almost dusk when she finally made her way
down to the road en route for the cottage. Stepping it
out, she scanned the route out from the port with an
occasional backward glance in the vague hope that
Verna might have been considerate enough to recall
that she had no transport, but there was no sign of the
hired car.

She had resigned herself to slogging it out for the
rest of the way when a car did approach from behind.
Where it had sprung from she had no idea, for the
road had certainly been deserted when she had last
turned. And it was not just any car. All her keyed-up
instincts were telegraphing to her the approach of
Rafael long before he came cruising alongside her, his
face oddly mask-like in the fading light.

'*Buenas tardes*, Miss Heatherton.' He opened the
door for her without first enquiring if she would care
for a lift. She hesitated, feeling that she had got the
worst over with, as regards the walk, and that it was

only a short way now to the cottage. But something about Rafael's steely charm made refusal somehow out of the question.

She felt those dark eyes watching her every move as she joined him in the car, and when they were on their way he said, his gaze on the road, 'The ankle—I see it is no longer troubling you, *señorita*.'.

'No.' She had the presence of mind to answer clearly. 'It's been work as usual today.'

'Of course. Work before everything, even injured limbs.' There was a satirical ring in his lighthearted comment. 'Yesterday you were crippled and could not come on the outing I had specially planned for you, but today, miraculously there is no trace of even a limp.'

'My work at the villa is not terribly strenuous, *señor*,' she fumbled for a reply. 'It's surprising what rest will do.'

'And your lunch hour and *siesta* period.' There was a kind of dangerous calm about him. 'Was that restful too, roaming the pathways of *el valle de los altramuces*?'

Terry's heart began to knock unevenly. So he had seen her in Lupin Valley! But how? Did he frequent it almost as much as she did? And had he watched her on other occasions too numerous to think of when she had thought she wandered there alone?

On another tack she said coolly, 'I hope the car outing was a success, *señor*.'

'The day went well,' he nodded noncommittally. It was only then, as she turned her head back to the window, sure that she had surmounted an awkward moment, that Terry saw they had overshot the avenue leading to the holiday estate and the cottage.

Her body tensing, she said steadily, 'I assumed I was accepting a lift home.'

'But why rush indoors?' Rafael's mouth sloped in menacing enquiry. 'Now that you have overcome—

shall we say, your indisposition—you are up to a little drive, are you not, to compensate for your absence among us yesterday?'

The speed with which he took the twisting mountain road to the Formentor peninsula convinced Terry that anything she said would have little effect on his present mood.

She felt wretched and miserable. To be found out in a small lie was bad enough. His contempt, and possibly his annoyance too for being deprived of the proud pleasure of showing off his beautiful island to her, was making him drive like someone possessed. But there was something else too, she felt, at the root of his grimly controlled attitude.

The sky had acquired that radiance of evening when the last of the sun's heat has drained away and the true blue that is left takes on a taffeta sheen. It lit the wildness and grandeur of their climb through the mountain pass where dizzying drops showed the white foam of green-blue seas licking at the base of the cliffs.

The savage scenery, Terry felt, could be likened to a man like Rafael; proud, commanding, ruthless at times, but always compelling.

Though the heights and depths of the drive were awe-inspiring she had no fears with Rafael in control. The more incensed he was, the saner his behaviour, she suspected, but she wished she knew what it was besides her shallow excuse to skip the car outing which had driven him to abducting her like this.

The sky was almost black when they stopped. Illuminated by brilliant stars and the slender crescent of a moon, the structure that Rafael was guiding her towards from the car, appeared medieval perched on the top of towering cliffs. She could hear the dull roar of the sea below and the high whine of the breeze among the rocky peaks.

The dark shape had a sentinel air, positioned as it was above the vast reaches of the night-shrouded sea. 'It is the *atalaya*,' Rafael told her, his face more than ever mask-like in the pale glow. 'A watch-tower built in the days of the Barbary pirates.'

'This is hardly the hour for a history lesson, is it?' said Terry, keeping her voice level.

'There is history past and present, Teresa,' Rafael said with a curious gleam in his eyes. 'That of the moment, for instance, when you can stand there looking demure and puzzled, knowing that the good name of the Villa Al Azhar is about to be rent asunder.'

His old-fashioned English would, at any other time, have caused Terry some amusement, but now she felt her heart lurch inside her at the implication of his words. What did he know? Had he discovered the awful truth about her and Verna? His next words seemed to discount this theory, though Terry experienced little relief, only further confusion as he added, 'You and *el chico* Chandler must be congratulating yourselves on the neat little sideline you have got going, *verdad*? It pays well, no, this selling of private information concerning the villa interior decor?'

Terry's blood ran cold. She had no idea what Rafael was talking about, but the mere mention of Leigh filled her with a familiar feeling of foreboding. Playing for time, she said, 'I haven't seen Leigh for several days.'

'The separation is perhaps bearable,' came the sneering reply, 'considering that it will be to your mutual advantage in the end.'

Terry was stuck for words. What had Leigh been up to now? She racked her brains trying to recall her last meeting with him. It was then that the terrible realisation hit her. That day on the headland overlooking Lupin Valley, they had talked about the villa a lot. In

fact Leigh had been obsessed with the subject. Her
heart began to thud. hollowly. Was it possible that
he——? *Selling private information concerning the villa
decor*. Rafael's words became emblazoned on her mind.

His gaze on her in the gloom was cold and contemp-
tuous. 'As Chandler is busy peddling his wares to new
villa owners up and down the coast,' he was saying
harshly, 'there will be little time for lovers' meetings.
After all the complete details of the Marqués del
Alcázar's dressing room, down to the last stud on the
wall, is—how do you say?—hot property to foolish
people who go in for this kind of sensationalism.' He
looked at her with the flicker of a change in his expression. 'You do not deny that you fed Chandler this
information during your meetings with him?'

'We talked on the subject ... yes,' Terry had to
admit. It was no good explaining that she had no idea
her disclosures would be exploited. Besides, Leigh was
in enough trouble as it was.

The trace of leniency in Rafael's expression was displaced by one of disappointment. 'I had hoped you
would deny the accusation, *señorita*. I believed that the
honesty that dwells in your gaze was the true indication
of your character. But I should have known,' his lip
curled, 'your sole concern is in Chandler's welfare.'

'It's true I've been worried about him since he came
out to the island with no money to live on,' Terry was
moved to reply, 'but we're not romantically attached
or ever likely to be.'

'*Claro que no!* But you don't mind helping him out
now and again with vital snippets of marketable
gossip.'

What could Terry say to this sceptically delivered
piece of sarcasm? She had talked to Leigh, and she had
described in detail her plans for Rafael's dressing
room. She didn't know there had been a motive behind

his sudden keen interest in the villa. But she ought to have guessed, knowing Leigh.

Her lack of replies were a continuing source of exasperation to Rafael. His jaw hardened. 'I would not have thought it possible,' he said, 'that you could repay Miss Wendell's kindness in accepting you as her apprentice by this kind of commercial treason. You must know that her ideas and design schemes are expressed in the strictest confidence, and it is this professional betrayal I find the most difficult to comprehend in your behaviour.'

Terry's face went white. It was one thing to be accused of talking freely about one's ideas, but when those ideas were believed to belong to someone else . . . But again, what could she say? She had allowed the deceit to ferment, and now how could she expect to escape Rafael's acute disgust?

In the vain hope she said, 'Aren't you making rather a lot out of one small incident—a conversation? Surely there are leaks of a certain nature, in every exclusive interior scheme planned?'

'If there are then in my case they will not be allowed to prosper,' he said in clipped tones. He viewed her with his steely, searching gaze. 'I could, of course, bring to light your conduct, but I wish to spare you this kind of distress. As for your young accomplice,' his voice tightened, 'he will make a little profit, but that is all.'

Terry said forlornly, 'Leigh never stays with one thing for long. I don't think you have much to worry about, *señor*.'

'You still continue to bleed for him.' Rafael was impatient. 'Yet you advised him against taking the position I offered him in the Marbella hotel.'

'You're wrong if you think that, *señor*.' Terry could at least contest this. 'I simply recognised that it was

his life and any straightening out to be done will have
to come from Leigh himself.'

Her resigned statement left a kind of void in the
conversation. For long enough the man beside her in
the starlight studied her through alternating moods.
Then in grinding frustration he expressed his thoughts.
'What is it about you, Teresa? Why do I always have
this feeling that you are afraid in some way? At first I
thought it was a dedication to your career which made
you so difficult to know, but that does not explain that
look of fright whenever I appear. Am I so tyrannical?
Have I made your life at the villa *insufrible* with my
appearances? Your every mood and thought is guarded
when I am around, and I am rapidly gathering the
conviction that it goes far beyond any feeling of concern for your work or even your childish anxiety for
the shiftless young Chandler, as I once suspected.
Admit to me that this is so, Teresa.'

Terry's face was ashen. Had she put it over as badly
as that? Rafael was a lot nearer than he realised to discovering the truth, and panicking, she blurted, 'I will
admit, if you wish, *señor*, that I am unhappy working
at the Villa Al Azhar, and since you've brought it up I
would like to leave—leave the island—tomorrow if
possible.'

Rafael's face took on a greyish pallor, but his smile
was twisted as he commented, 'So! You can leave all
your pet accomplishments, just like that! You have no
feeling of affinity with that you have helped to create?
You can walk away from the villa and its imminent
unfolding as a home of grace and beauty with not even
a pang in your heart for what it has become?'

Terry stifled a sob in her throat. She knew in herself
that leaving the Villa Al Azhar was going to be the
greatest wrench in her life. Unlike any other job she
had worked on, a part of herself had gone into its crea-

tion and that part of her would remain, no matter
where she travelled over the face of the earth to forget
the house and its owner. The anguish of being forever
incomplete made her fly at him with the remark, 'Do
we have to have an analysis study simply because I
want to leave my place of employment——?'

Rafael's keen glance was raking her face and with a
trace of triumph in his manner he grabbed her by the
shoulders. 'So I am right! The Villa Al Azhar has a
hold on you. It has a special meaning for you, just as it
has for me. You will not easily turn your back on it
despite your desperation to pretend otherwise.'

Terry struggled in his grasp. 'Everyone gets a little
attached to something they ... have had a hand in,'
she blustered. 'And anyway, there's very little work
left now for an ... assistant to——'

'You will remain until the villa interiors are completed.' His fingers sank into her flesh. 'Miss Wendell
may be your immediate superior, but I have ultimate
control over the work-force under my roof, and you
will not terminate your duties until I give my permission.'

Terry slumped, became almost acquiescent in his
grip. What was the point in arguing? Rafael had the
whip hand. Autocratic and masterful, he could always
be counted on to demonstrate his strength when
necessary. And anyway, Verna wouldn't take too
kindly to the thought of her leaving. Not until she had
finished off the last of the design schemes for the villa.

An odd kind of situation arose there in the starlight
beside the *atalaya*. Terry had thought that because she
offered no resistance to his demands Rafael would let
her go. But his hands continued to grip her shoulders,
though with less intensity. Had she wanted to she could
have turned out of his grasp, but some sweet compulsion held her there. And while she knew it was danger-

ous to linger no part of her could resist the weakening magnetism of his nearness.

Afraid to show anything of the pleasurable tumult taking place within her in those palpitating seconds, she turned her gaze to run it over the dark bulk of the watch-tower. Conscious of her every flicker of movement, her every breath, it seemed to her, Rafael said, 'You are interested in the other history, *señorita*? That of the Barbary pirates?'

'I was thinking,' Terry worked to keep her voice steady. 'You picked me up on the road and drove me to this wild and desolate spot with no warning, *señor*.'

'This is Spain,' his dark eyes glowed strangely. 'In many ways we are primitives.'

Something about the moment brought it flashing into her mind, that enigmatic question that Rafael had put to her that day in Lupin Valley. *What would you do if you were abducted to some lonely bell-tower retreat?*

There was a slight twist to his lips which told her he knew her thoughts. His gaze was molten, almost tender, and wholly hypnotic. Terry was held by it, her heart behaving like an imprisoned bird in her chest. Then his mouth came down hard on hers.

The move was not unexpected, yet Terry had done nothing to avoid it. It was as though this moment had been decreed from the very beginning of her life and to hold aloof would have been like putting an end to the sweetness of one's existence. Rafael's arms were unyielding, his embrace almost brutal; there was something vitally demanding in the way his lips explored hers. And all of this she had no armour against. How could she have, when she loved him so? To steal a little of something which could never be hers might be madness, but all the will power in the world couldn't get her to see that now.

Passion can be a frightening thing when bared in

oneself for the first time, and, aflame under the fire of Rafael's caressing lips, she knew it was the reminder that the drive here and subsequent exchanges had taken place in an atmosphere of acute animosity. This was what came to her aid in the end. Rafael was angry, and men did peculiar things when they were angry. He was the master now, there was no doubt, but he might have picked a less disturbing way to prove it.

Aghast now at having given herself away so completely, she wrenched away from the ecstasy of his nearness with such suddenness she almost overbalanced. As he steadied her against the wall of the watch-tower Rafael's dark gaze locked with hers. With a touch of triumph in his voice he asked, 'And what do you have to say now, Teresa?'

Twisting in an effort to avoid his look, his expression which somehow tugged at her heart, she choked with a rush, 'I still want to leave—now—tonight—as soon as I can——'

His face greyed over. That half-triumphant smile on his lips became bent, and after a moment he said with a weary kind of gentleness, 'You are afraid I am serious in my intention to keep you locked away here in the *atalaya*. Have no fear, child, the stone walls and bare floor of a lonely watch-tower are hardly the trappings I would choose for your abduction. But you will stay on the island, as I have said, until your work at the villa is finished.'

With a hand on her arm he steered her to the car, and in reply to her frantic desire to escape from him and the island which he read so clearly in her eyes he repeated, 'You will stay.'

CHAPTER TEN

IN a week's time Rafael was going to a bankers' meeting in Bilbao, in the north of Spain, and was expected to be away several days. Terry didn't see how it was possible to round things off at the villa in so short a time, but she vowed to herself that while he was away she would disappear, flee from the island and out of his life for ever. Verna would be quite capable of tying up the loose ends at the villa, and if she married Rafael, Terry thought bleakly, she would have a whole lifetime to do it.

If he did one day discover the truth about their fraudulent partnership he would be sufficiently softened by marriage to smile away Verna's deceit. As for her own, Terry thought, hollow-eyed, she would be no more than a dim memory in his mind by then, and not of sufficient interest to rouse deep feelings other than distaste. But there was still a week to go and somehow she had to struggle through it, pretending that work at the villa was the paramount thing.

The July heat was stunning. It was impossible to work through the somnolent hours between twelve and four, and shunning the beach now, so close to the hotel terrace and Rafael and his friends, Terry sought the cool shade of Lupin Valley and swam on the lonely stretch of beach at its outlet.

She worked long hours into the evening at the villa, taking advantage of the cooler period and the fact that the place was devoid of workmen at this hour. But so too did the visitors to Al Azhar prefer the cool and the quiet. Rafael and Verna dropped in regularly. Things had reached such a pitch with the designing work that it hardly mattered, Terry thought slackly, that she appeared to be doing everything about the place. It was only what she had been used to on other assignments, and Verna had grown into the mould of playing the figurehead who did very little of the actual manual side of designing; a guise which she wore well in Rafael's company.

Since the night on the cliff beside the *atalaya* Terry had not spoken to the Marqués except in the capacity of assistant when they discussed some point on the particular layout of a room. Her voice was quiet and polite and she felt his eyes on her on these occasions, willing her to meet his gaze, but she had done that once before, with disastrous results. Also she knew his glances were searching, which terrified her, for wasn't he already suspicious that there was something that caused her deep unease?

His presence at the villa was a source of constant torment to her. But worse in another sense was the arrival of Miriam's mother on the scene. Rosa Perez had expressed a desire to tour the almost completed villa and Rafael obligingly drove her up on one of his trips with Verna.

Terry had never forgotten her ordeal under the questing surveillance of Señora Perez that night when the woman had invited her to her hotel suite. But though Rosa eyed her keenly with that mind-boring scrutiny of hers, she was chatty and openly delighted at all she saw at the villa. Terry trailed round dutifully at the rear, listening to her Spanish exclamations of pleasure and happy surprise. She was acutely observing, noting the fine detail in a wall-side bureau, the eggshell fragility of a glass-flower-framed mirror. She approved of the masculine flavour given to the library and Rafael's private rooms, and had only one overall complaint, issued laughingly, that she was resident in Madrid and could only spend brief sessions on the island. Rafael was both charming and attentive towards the older woman. Rosa Perez was not one to give praise lightly, but there was no saying what his private thoughts were on Rosa's presumption that he would marry her daughter.

In the grand *salón* she noticed at once the golden warmth of the room. 'Now this is what I would call my *sala de verano*,' she exclaimed. 'It is so like summer I can almost hear the buzzing of the *abejas* among the foliage on the drapes.' She turned to the Marqués with an almost accusing gleam. 'You realise, Rafael, you have all the *estaciones* of the year under your roof. *El pequeño salón*, so springlike, the sunshine bursts of colour here, the coppery decor of the terrace lounge and your own quarters cosy and intimate as any Madrid fireside when those nasty *sierra* winds blow.'

It took a woman like Rosa Perez to notice what could well have been overlooked in the general viewing of the villa. There were many rooms and each had its own mood, but Rosa had spotted what Terry had vaguely hoped to achieve in her overall thinking concerning design. There *was* a seasonal aspect about the rooms mentioned, but it was hearing it put into words by an outsider which brought it home to Terry just how successful her ideas had turned out.

Of course she kept her lashes lowered, while Verna, fawning in this instance for Señora Perez' high opinions of the villa decor, would set the seal on her own chances with the Marqués, hung on to her every word. After a moment or two Terry felt safe amidst the chat, then some stab of unease told her that Rafael was no longer listening to the conversation. As far as she knew she had given nothing away in her expression after Rosa's revelations, yet she couldn't shake off the feeling that momentarily she was the sole object of his attention, and as she raised her gaze he looked at her long and hard.

Luckily Rosa's presence in the villa was an all-commanding one and the tour continued until she had seen every corner, inside and out, and proclaimed her approval. Rafael, courteous and considerate, accompanied her everywhere, and it was he who escorted her solicitously to his car at the conclusion of the visit. She smiled, taking his warm concern as her due, but of Verna's added company on the drive back to the hotel she was haughtily disapproving.

Terry had never been more relieved to see anyone depart from the villa. Rosa Perez had bloodhound qualities when something intrigued her, and though she had not openly studied Terry during the visit, Terry always felt that she had eyes in the back of her head when her nervousness was in danger of showing.

But soon now the nightmare would be over. That evening she learned from Verna that for the next three days Rafael would be entertaining banking officials in his suite at the hotel and after that would accompany them to Bilbao. He expected to be gone about a week, but Terry intended to wait no longer than receiving the news that he had left by plane to slip away herself from the island. Of course she said nothing to anyone about her plans, least of all Verna. Her partner would hardly be likely to miss her at this stage when her ambitions were almost certain to be fulfilled, and once in England she would disappear so completely no one would find her.

She estimated that what she had to do for her own artistic satisfaction at the villa could be completed within the next three days. After that Verna would no doubt derive another kind of satisfaction from putting the finishing touches to the place. It would mean putting in long hours at Al Azhar and in the present heat it would be particularly taxing, especially as she had become a shadow of herself these past days and felt too sapped with despondency to cope.

It wasn't exactly a rosy time to receive visitors. Not that Terry expected to see Rosa Perez again. But it was she who appeared in the doorway of the villa that following morning. And what made it more ominous, she was entirely alone.

'I left my chauffeur with the car parked on the slope of the *camino*,' she explained cheerfully. 'I felt a little exercise would be good for my ageing limbs.'

There appeared to be little senile about the *señora* at the moment, least of all her regard, which was as piercing as ever.

'*Ay que maravilloso es este vestibulo!*' Often lapsing into Spanish, she gazed about her as though with fresh and renewed interest.

Terry had been having slight trouble with the vestibule. High-ceilinged and spacious, it communicated directly with the main *salón*, of which there was an ample view. Its walls were white, its floor of Majorcan russet tiles. It had a central stone fountain of greenery, and a marble pedestal holding a finely sculptured head stood to the side of the opening into the *salón*. On each side of the typical large stone fireplace she had placed, facing the centre of the room, two high-backed basket-work chairs of ornate contemporary design, and these were complemented by carpet-sized woven straw mats one on either side of the fountain. Green plants decorated the walls at random and Terry had been racking her brain for days wondering what it was the vestibule needed to give it that crowning touch. It was unfortunate that she had hit on the very thing just at Rosa Perez' arrival and had been rapidly transferring her thoughts to paper. Now the almost completed sketch showed a canework mesh fitment which would cover the whole ceiling at a slightly lower level, adding a warmth to the vestibule, and allowing vines and other greenery to twine among the canework, eventually giving a leafy effect overhead.

'*Vaya!*' Rosa picked up the sketch and eyed it closely. 'I did not know you were so clever with a pencil.'

Terry shrugged, conscious of the eagle gaze fixed on her. 'I'm simply following up Miss Wendell's ideas, of course.'

'For the *vestíbulo*?' The *señora*'s eyebrows lifted. 'Does she intend to make additions here?'

'I think . . .' Terry struggled to appear offhand, 'she does have something in mind.'

Rosa was looking at her in a strange way. Her eyes piercingly on target, she said, 'I find that very odd. On the drive back to the hotel Miss Wendell gave me to understand that her work was finished here.'

'Then . . . then,' Terry stumbled, 'she must have had a change of heart.'

'Between the time she left us at the hotel at midnight last night and now?' Señora Perez' regard was even more curious.

'I'm . . . just an assistant,' Terry floundered. Telling an untruth while being nailed by that ferreting black gaze was the hardest thing in the world for her.

'An assistant with *talento abundante*.' Her questing attitude relaxing slightly, Rosa studied the sketch with admiration and asked, 'Tell me, Miss Heatherton, where did you learn to capture so completely a brilliant idea?'

'I've told you,' Terry replied weakly, 'I . . . only follow orders. It's . . . up to me to tie up any necessary ends here and that's what I'm doing . . . so if you don't mind . . .' she reached out a hand for the telltale sketchbook, 'I'll . . . er . . . get on with the job.'

Rosa handed her the pad. 'Rafael will like it,' she said with a sudden smile. 'I am sure of it.' But it was a smile that soon hardened around the edges. She wandered about the vestibule and later the *salón*, and Terry had the nerve-racking feeling that she was relating all she saw there with what she had seen on the sketchpad.

The house was eerily silent. The only sound came from a sunny terrace at the rear where workmen were laying the last of the swimming pool tiles. Head bent, Terry pretended to be vitally engrossed in measurement figures, and at last Rosa returned to the open entrance, ready to leave. But before she started out down the drive where her chauffeur and car were waiting round the bend she said, viewing Terry with one of her sagacious looks, 'Verna has never struck me as being a sensitive type. Whereas you, child, everything about you says you have a temperament *ascetica*.'

Terry was faint with nerves once the woman had left. But it was all that was needed to spur her into action. She had had enough of Rosa Perez' prying ways. She would pack her bags and get off the island without wasting any more time. She knew a firm at the port who could make the canework mesh for the vestibule ceiling. They could no doubt make it in a day if she stressed that speed was important, and then she would have to supervise the fitting for her own peace of mind. But after that nothing would induce her to remain at the villa where she had given all she had in her heart to its creation and only a wraith of herself survived to make the getaway.

Within minutes she was hurtling into town in the hired car, and all went well at the canework firm. The manager grasped her requirements speedily and promised workmen on the job before the day was out. The whole exercise, he was confident, would take no more than a couple of days. Terry would have preferred to see it finished in less time, but quality, she knew, could not be rushed. And one thing was certain. The moment Rafael stepped on to that plane for Bilbao she would be booking her own flight into obscurity.

Pale and worn, her mind full of all she must do to close the tracks behind her when she left, she barely heard the shout from close by as she took a short cut along a back street towards the car. 'Hey, Terry!' A little breathless, Leigh caught up with her and when he was alongside he asked, 'Where's the fire? Don't you get time to acknowledge old friends these days?'

'Oh, hello, Leigh,' Terry said lifelessly. 'I'm sorry, but I am in a bit of a hurry.'

'Whoops! Air's a bit chilly around here.' He eyed her closely but in no way sheepishly, then snapped his fingers. 'Oh, I get it. You've heard about the Marqués' private pad lark.'

'I really don't want to discuss it,' Terry said coldly.

Leigh looked about him, spotted an open courtyard at the rear of a hotel where tables and chairs were set in the shade. 'Let's have a drink,' he suggested. At Terry's lack of response he added rather more earnestly, 'I want to talk to you, Terry. I'm leaving the island.'

She silently consented then, her glance full of enquiry. The courtyard on the back street running parallel with the sea front was a haven of shade and peace and quiet. A twin flight of stone steps flanking the ironwork doorway was decorated with flowering pots and a smooth-boled fig tree offered respite from the fierce sun. There were many of these jewel-like arbours situated along the side-alleys of the port, Terry reflected spiritlessly.

After they had been served with drinks Leigh said with a twist of ironic humour about his lips, 'You'll be pleased to know that I'm about to disappear, get out of your hair, as it were.' He scotched any leaping of Terry's heart by adding, 'Me and a mate of mine are off to Italy. There's a big thing going in the art galleries in Florence. The tourists flock there in the thousands—not just in the summer, right?—and we reckon that speaking the lingo a bit we'll do all right giving our version of the motheaten masterpieces.'

Her eyes no longer full of hurt, Terry asked in a downhearted voice, 'Is that really what you want to do, Leigh?'

'Trust a woman to throw cold water on a good idea!' he joked with a crooked grin, but the light in his eyes bordered on the penitent. 'Look, Terry,' he said with a rush, 'I didn't mean to play the louse, pumping you for information on the villa. It was just that it was a good thing at the time, you understand. A guy has to make a living . . .'

Terry had only to raise her gaze to bring it on a level with his, and in exasperated discomfort he burst out beneath his breath, 'Oh, hell! What's the use? You might as well know the truth. I'm leaving anyway.' Taking a breath, he smiled with a trace of his delinquent bravado and began, 'I was on my uppers in London when you told me you were about to do a job for the Marqués del Alcázar. I figured with a title like that he'd be worth a packet, so I got myself over here to Pollensa with a view to soaking him for a bit, through you, of course. I had no definite plans, I just thought something would turn up where I would come off big. But the ideas got kind of grounded.

'I told you the Marqués offered me a job when he took me for a drive that night, but I didn't let you in on the whole of the lecture. He doesn't beat about the

bush, doesn't our Raf de Quiso. He made it known
that he was on to my trailing you here to the island for
no-good reasons. He said—putting it like a gentleman—I'd have to watch my step. He also said that if I
hurt you in any way I'd have to answer to him. Well,
after that things became a bit sticky. What could I do?
Anything involving you was out. I mean, the Marqués is
not a man—as the old ladies would say—to mince words.'

Hardly confronting his braggart humour, Terry
asked, 'And what about the dressing-room episode?'

Leigh shrugged with a bitter gleam. 'Don't think I
was going to let the Marqués have it all his own way. I
decided he'd pay for his superior scuttling of my plans
somehow, and filching his dressing-room details gave
me a kick. The idea would have gone a bomb, but the
estate agents wouldn't touch it after the Marq's lawyers
had had a go at them. Still, I picked up a bit. Made
my fare to spaghetti land.'

With despair and affection mingling with the rueful
smile in her eyes, Terry asked, 'And when do you leave
for Italy?'

'Tonight. We're taking the ferry to Gerona and
hitch-hiking from there. This is it, Terry. Goodbye, I
mean. Running into you like this has saved me making
a trip to the villa.' The fact that he had intended to
search her out before he left said something for their
relationship, and recognising this he put out a hand
and clasped hers with a kind of ironic affection. 'You
make it rough on a guy who has to live by his wits.'

'Leigh,' she hung on to his grasp for a second, 'will
it always be like that?'

'Who knows?' he shrugged, rising and tossing a
peseta note down for the drinks. 'One day I might
polish the seat of a chair in some fancy office—if there's
one going in the year 2000.' With his indolent grin he
left her and went strolling off down the back street,

whistling the catchy pop tune that was the current rage in Spain.

Terry sat for a moment, saddened by his going but recognising it as inevitable. Leigh would always be on the move, always looking for the peace of mind that he pretended so bravely he could do without, and which he would find in the end in his own heart.

The day of Rafael's departure arrived. Terry had her bags packed in her room, but after seeing him off from the hotel Verna was excited at the thought of the villa being near enough complete and insisted on seeing everything now that they could talk together without fear of being found out.

She made no secret of her irritation at the timing of the business trip. If it hadn't been for this dreary banking conference she might by now be wearing Rafael's engagement ring. And Terry knew that she only wanted to go to the Villa Al Azhar to view it undisturbed and picture herself as the mistress of it.

Terry had no choice but to accompany her in the hired car later in the day, even though she knew that Rafael would now be well ensconced in Bilbao and the sand had already begun to trickle through the hourglass measuring her chances of escape. But it occurred to her that it would be no easy task either breaking away from Verna, who showed that she was tenaciously of the opinion that Terry should remain until she had no further use for her. This being the case, it might be wiser to leave the cottage around the midnight hour when Verna was in her room.

At the present moment, with the sun streaming in the car windows, night-time seemed an eternity away and exhausted by the stress of these past days Terry knew she must hang on till then somehow.

Verna was pleased with the canework ceiling fitment

in the vestibule—as pleased as she could be about things that didn't come into her actual orbit of thinking. She strolled around eyeing the decor in an abstract way, a woman moved by nothing except the force of her own desires.

'If you want you can carry on with the tidying up,' she said, waving a hand to Terry. 'Don't mind me. I'm going to amuse myself looking round the bedrooms.'

Once she had disappeared Terry supposed wearily that she might as well try to finish off a problem corner she had been working on. Anything to make the time go quicker. All the things were on hand; it was simply a matter of arranging them in a satisfactory way.

She had known what she wanted for this corner in the reception room, but the fact that it housed a doorway on either side leading to other apartments had left her with doubts as to the practicability of her original plan. She had chosen a quite beautiful escritoire of bow-shaped design. Black and gold with tiny inlaid-pearl pattern at the sides, it was neat and compact but didn't look happy alongside either wall. Of course a corner should have something to fill it, she knew. But then the gold-framed pictures she had lined up looked all wrong. She hadn't realised that there was going to be an awkward gap no matter how she arranged the petite escritoire.

For long enough she surveyed the empty corner, picturing in her mind the pieces that stood by waiting to be finally positioned. In her spiritless state she had little feeling for the artistic, but then, as always when she became lost in the pursuit of an idea, something clicked. Of course—that was it! The ebony and gold claw-footed plant holder that she had known would be an asset to a room but had found no definite place for. She had only filled it with flowers yesterday.

Hurrying off, she soon had it alongside her other items and with a surge of confidence she set to work. *Now* it all fitted—the huge gold-framed picture filling up the broadest expanse of cherry-pink wall on the right and flatteringly edged by the broad white and black-bordered doorway frame and skirting board. And the smaller gold-framed picture with its own light attachment on the narrower shadowed wall on the left and a miniature gold-bordered etching beneath. Now the escritoire, topped with gold-stemmed cream silk lampshade and two tiny gold figurines, could go at right angles here, and that problematical gap—with a flourish Terry placed the ebony and gold based flower arrangement on the floor beside the right-hand opening. The arc-shaped pastel-tinted spray sparkled against the lower expanse of cherry wall, and looking at it framed by the black and white woodwork of doorway and skirting board, she knew it was a master touch.

Standing back to survey her work, she experienced the familiar thrill of a job well done. The effect was superb, there was no denying—and with the old heartache starting up again—she couldn't have wished to leave a more appropriate parting gift for Rafael's return.

She had only been standing away a second or two and pleasure still filled her at her handiwork when a sound broke the utter silence of the room. It was that of someone clapping discreetly, and Terry spun round to find Rosa Perez seated quite comfortably on a settee beside the open french windows.

'*Exquisito!* You work with the sensitivity of the true artist, Teresa.'

Any vestige of colour that remained in Terry's face after her days of ordeal drained away at the sight of Rosa. The agonising questions flew into her mind.

How long had she been sitting there? How much had she seen?

Reading her thoughts as always, Rosa explained obligingly, 'I saw your car on the drive and walked round to make an unnoticed entry. I wanted to see for myself just how the Al Azhar's interior designer works when she is alone.'

'*Señora*—what I was doing just now——' On the point of collapse from the shock of being discovered, so lost had she been in her vocation, Terry battled in vain to come up with some feasible excuse for her actions.

'—Bears the stamp of all that has been so perfectly executed in other rooms,' Rosa finished for her. 'That a mere apprentice could rise to such symmetry of arrangement I find difficult to believe, *señorita*.'

'I hardly think it matters what you believe, *señora*.' Chalk white, Terry made a show of being indifferent. 'As an assistant here to a——'

'So you still persist,' Señora Perez rose and advanced, 'in trying to fob me off with that *chiste* when I have seen examples on more than one occasion of the gifted artist you are.'

'I really don't know what you're talking about.' Frantically Terry looked round for a means of escape. 'And if you insist on interrupting my duties then I shall have no choice but to go elsewhere to——'

'*Señorita*.' Rose Perez grasped her arm, her eyes like pebbles in ice. 'There is something going on here, and I mean to get to the bottom of it. I have known for some time that Verna is a sham, but in what way I have been unable to *verificar*. Now, since my talks with you, and the way I have watched you. *Pero si!* What I have seen here this afternoon convinces me that the two of you are engaged in some kind of *duplicidad*.'

Terry fancied that she heard a sound just beyond

the reception room doorway, but it could have been the pounding of her own heart and the rushing of blood in her ears. She didn't know which way to turn. Her nerves at snapping point from living with the lie too long, she had no defences against the indomitable Spanish matron except to ridicule feebly, 'What you're implying, *señora*, is beyond me. Really! I come here to follow instructions——'

'What are you afraid of, Teresa?' Rosa suddenly thrust her face close. 'What is it that haunts you?—I have seen it in your eyes.'

'Will you please leave me alone!' Terry all but screamed, and stumbled towards the open french windows. She could think of nowhere more blissful to hide from that prying gaze than Lupin Valley, and within minutes she had found the path and was hurrying swayingly up the incline to the ridge gateway.

Once she was through she was compelled to stop, for the sobs in her throat were interfering with her breathing. She needed time to gather strength; enough to lose herself in the comforting seclusion of all she loved here.

But the pause turned out to have a blood-chilling significance. It set the scene for a horrifying enactment that had she known she would have lurched away, on hands and knees if necessary, to put distance between herself and that chasm-like drop where the ridge fell away beside the gateway.

But no one knows what lies ahead and Terry was too concerned in fleeing from the past. Rosa Perez, on the other hand, had her daughter's future with Rafael to think of. She was looking for something with which to discredit Verna in his eyes and, so near the truth, like a woman possessed, she was hot on Terry's trail.

The confrontation took place there beside the gateway into Lupin Valley. 'Teresa!' Rosa gasped, also

breathing heavily, for she was no longer a young
woman. 'You will tell me everything. Can you not see,
child, it is pointless to try and deny what I can see so
clearly for myself. You and Verna are a partnership,
but it is you we must thank for the interior decor at Al
Azhar. Am I not right?' Seeing Terry's utter and total
prostration, she hounded on, 'If you will not confess
to this, at least acknowledge that Verna does not know
the first thing about house design and that her talent,
as I suspected from the start, lies in her ability to
impress.'

Terry shot her a frightened look which must have
been eloquent enough, for after eyeing her for several
seconds Rosa flung back her head and gave a victorious
laugh. 'So it is all true! Our Miss Wendell who preens
along with the well-to-do at the Hotel Esperanza is
nothing but a hoax, a *tramposa*! *Vaya! Vaya!* Wait
until Rafael hears about this!'

'All right, nosy Rosa.' There was a sound from the
gateway and suddenly Verna appeared. Gone now was
her svelte assurance, her smooth finesse. Her lips were
drawn back from a smile which in a face that was waxen
and shrunken was almost demoniacal. 'I'm sick of your
busybodying ways, do you know that?' That she had
overheard all that had gone on in the house and up
here was obvious as she advanced. 'Sick and tired of
your spying, snooping ways! I've had you breathing
down the back of my neck for too long. You never let
up, Rosa. But if you think I'm going to let you disrupt
all I've painstakingly set up for myself by running to
Rafael with what your incessant meddling has turned
up, then you don't know me as well as you thought
you did!' Her voice became coarse and high-pitched.
'You may be feeling pleased at the moment, Rosa, but
I can promise you it won't last. You forget,' she
suddenly grasped the older woman by the arms and

forced her off the path, 'once a cheat, always a cheat.'

Terry, still out of breath, both emotionally and with the dash from the house, reacted dazedly at first and then with a horrifying realisation. 'Verna! In heaven's name, what are you doing!'

Rosa too, with no physical stamina left, could only stare, blank-faced, as she felt herself going backwards towards the steep slope beyond the path.

'You keep out of this!' With elephantine strength Verna went on pushing. 'I haven't come this far to let either of you rob me of what's mine.'

'Verna! Are you mad?' Terry grasped Rosa's arm and held on while she gazed with terror-stricken enquiry at the other girl. 'There's a hundred-foot drop down there!'

'Shut—*up*!' Verna continued to thrust the woman before her. As the ground fell away from her heels Rosa could only croak out a stunned cry of protest.

In the struggle Terry felt herself slipping towards the incline. Spent with their emotional wrangling, both she and Rosa were a puny match for Verna who, obsessed with all that was at stake for her, was imbued with superhuman strength.

While she held on to firm ground Terry knew her own grip on a level footing was fast receding. But still she hung on to Rosa. The woman's face glazed now with a kind of helpless horror aroused in her acute compassion. She pleaded with her eyes for help and Terry gave it to her, at grim cost to herself.

The older woman, losing her balance as the ground dropped away, fell abruptly into space and Terry, crying to the coldly smiling Verna to stop this idiocy before it was too late, was tugged along by the momentum of Rosa's fall out too into that green vacuum.

She heard the woman's scream, and that other

sound, coming from a long way off, must have been her own.

Rolling, rolling—it was like threshing in a demon world where rocks and grass played punishing tricks and leafy ledges offered no respite from the downward hurl. Terry knew only that she had lost her grip on Rosa, and then the blackness closed in.

CHAPTER ELEVEN

THAT grey, painful world that seemed to go on and on was lit by blurred movement. Shadowy figures passing by an inner vision belonged to a ghostly sect, and anxious voices echoed and boomed in a mind that was disembodied and belonged nowhere.

For long enough, aeons in time, it floated above the pain and the muddle, and then the blurs became colour ... rose pink ... deep rose pink ... pale rose pink—roses—roses!

Beneath her eyelids Terry was aware of the hues taking shape, slowly as her lashes lifted she discovered there were roses everywhere; on the pillows, on the coverlet. With tears of weakness in her eyes she recognised this room. Hadn't she devised this plain rose-pink canopy pleated to ceiling height against the wall of the rose-sprigged bedhead and draped with matching rose-sprigged frills? And hadn't she had made the huge similarly patterned sofa, soft and feminine, and placed it alongside the wall-length picture-windows; the curtains too a cascade of ceiling to floor length roses on a flower-sprigged background, drawn now to shut out the bright sunlight. They were as she had devised them.

She turned her head to take in more and let out a small whimper as a pain shot down her neck. But it passed in a moment and then she saw the vase of roses, pink and white and sprigged with cool, starry jasmine. How quiet and still was the room! And now that shaft of hurt brought everything back to her—the precipitous slope above the ridge drop; herself and Rosa strug-

gling to hang on, the woman's screams—it was all so
terrifyingly real she almost sat up. It was a comfort to
know that she could just about attempt it, but her body
was a mass of aches and the pillow beckoned invitingly
to her throbbing head.

The door opened then and the figure of a nurse
appeared. Plump and dark-haired, she beamed at the
bed, *'Gracias a Dios! Esta consciente. Como esta, peque-
ña?'* Chattering away in Spanish, she smoothed the hair
back from Terry's forehead, crimped her pillows,
smoothed her sheets and went out.

Seconds later someone else appeared in the doorway.
'Terry darling! We thought you were never going to
open your eyes again! How are you, dear?' Verna
trilled.

Rafael followed her in. *Rafael*, taut-faced, unsmiling
but with a gentle light in his eyes. 'So you are with us
again, Teresa.' His voice lacked its usual strong timbre.
'We were beginning to think your coma was more
serious than we were given to believe.'

'How . . . long have I been here?' Her own voice
sounded strange to her and talking to Rafael it
quavered more than it should have done.

'Three days.' He came to the bed. 'Before that you
were in the clinic at Alcudia. You were a mass of con-
tusions and a temple bruise caused prolonged concus-
sion. But as soon as I was assured that you were not
seriously injured I had you brought to Al Azhar.'

'And . . .' Terry asked, unable to keep the tremble
from her throat, '. . . Doña Rosa Perez?'

'She too survived the fall. A blow on the head has
left her with severe amnesia. She remembers nothing
of her life before the accident, but her doctors are confident she will recuperate with time. Miriam has
returned with her to Madrid.'

At this Terry met Verna's gaze. She could see now

why her partner was so bright and smiling, if a little watchful. She had nothing to fear now from Rosa, and Miriam had gone too. The way was more than clear to push on with her wedding plans. *And Rafael would never know the truth.* If Rosa Perez recovered her faculties with convalescence it would make little difference, for Verna would by then be the Marquesa del Alcázar.

All this was written in the brilliant look she gave Terry.

But Rafael was watching Terry too and, aware of those dark eyes measuring her every reaction both to his and to Verna's presence in the room, she asked to fill the silence, 'Your business trip . . . I thought you were in Bilbao?'

'Of course I flew straight home when I heard what happened,' Rafael said grimly. 'Fernando the chauffeur came to the villa from the car that afternoon to remind Señora Perez of an approaching tea appointment she had with friends at the hotel. He heard the screams up near the ridge gateway. It was he who gave the alarm.'

Because Rafael's eyes never stopped searching her face while he spoke Terry could only murmur, weakly apologetic, 'Your bankers' meeting . . . I'm sorry if all this has——'

'It is of little importance to me, Teresa.' His words cut across her whispered digressions with a force that showed rigid control. Then in softer tones he went on, 'Believe me, I do not like having to put you through this unpleasantness when you have suffered so much, but what is important to me now is knowing just what happened up there by the valley entrance. What was Señora Perez doing beside the ridge gateway? She is not a woman to indulge in country walks. And how was it that she and yourself came to be so near the slope edge—more than a comfortable distance from the path—that you both went over the side?'

'As I've explained to Rafael,' Verna cut in with a hard message in her eyes, 'you and Rosa were having some kind of difference of opinion. I don't know whether you intended to browbeat her so far away from the path, or whether it was just your hold on her that made her lose her balance ... I mean ... I can only describe what I saw.'

Terry knew a need to lower her lashes over the bruised shadows under her eyes to weather the electric shock of Verna's words. So that was how she had absolved herself from any blame! She was innocently making out that she, Terry, had argued with Rosa, that she could have pushed her over the edge and in doing so had lost her own balance.

She suddenly felt deathly weary. Why bother to stir up the pain? Nothing mattered any more. It didn't matter that she was disgraced. She would be leaving anyhow. And Verna could start her life at the Villa Al Azhar with a nice clean page. But it was leaving with this kind of stigma. *That Rafael should think that of her!* That was what cut deep. She shot a look at him. And he was there to receive it, to weigh it, and view with silent enquiry the inner wound that he saw in her eyes. With words he asked, 'Is that true, Teresa? Was there some kind of disagreement between you and Rosa Perez?'

Terry felt the pillow growing damp beneath her head. Oh, she was clever, was Verna. How accurately she had spun her tale so it was an almost perfect fit. Terry *had* had words with Rosa. And she *had* been desperate to rid herself of the woman. But not in the way that Verna had implied. But who would ever know that now? *Or believe it?*

Running up against the other girl's brilliantly

assured gleam, she said faintly, 'I ... don't want to talk about it.'

'Why don't we leave it, Rafael?' Verna came in with insolicitous tones. 'Poor Terry is entitled to withhold her reasons for the ... fracas, as no real harm's been done. After all, Rosa is on the mend and heaven knows Terry's paid in a way for her ... er ... rash mood. Perhaps all she wants now is peace and quiet.'

Rafael, whose expression bordered on the thoughtful at Verna's hard, bright eagerness to let the matter drop, nodded in agreement after a moment. 'Very well.' He sat down suddenly on the side of the bed and took Terry's hand in his. 'It is not my wish to put you through more *dolor*. If that is what you want we will forget the episode. Now all that remains is for you to get well again.'

He rose just as abruptly and turned. 'Verna, the atmosphere of the past days has hardly been one with which to herald the completion of the villa. But as your work has long been finished here I see no reason why you should not return now to your own country.'

Verna's mouth dropped open. The permanent smile there froze into a kind of mystified question mark. 'But, Rafael ... I mean ... don't we have things to discuss?'

'All business talk to do with payment for interior design services can be conducted at a later date in London,' Rafael said pleasantly. 'I am sure you must be keen to start on a new *asignación* now that there is nothing to keep you here. Naturally I will make all arrangements for your departure for England.'

Verna was rooted at this swift dispensing of, not just her services, but of her person. She stared at the bedside as though still seeing Rafael sitting there holding Terry's hand, and the coarseness came through as she asked, 'And what about her?'

'Teresa will stay here until she is well,' Rafael said.
'And then what?'

'And then we will talk.'

'Talk? What about?' Verna's high-pitched tones cracked.

'Who knows, Verna? Who knows?' His smile sloped tiredly, after which he looked briskly at his watch. 'But for now I must go. I am needed at the hotel. The manager is having difficulties with an influx of new arrivals. I do not expect to see you again before you leave the island, Verna, so I will take this opportunity of wishing you goodbye and *adios*.' With a bow he left the room.

The silence he left behind was thunderous. Only the sound of his footsteps departing broke the unnatural stillness. Moments later there was the throb of his car engine starting up on the drive. All the noisy manoeuvring of the wheels being steered towards the paved incline bounced around the walls of the interior, then it was moving away, taking the last vestige of normality from the room as the hum of the engine slowly receded and faded away in the distance.

'Why, you little creep!' Verna's face had shrunk to rabbit-like ferocity. 'So *you're* the one who's been quietly milking Rafael's attention!' She moved in with menacing fury. 'I should have known! And under my nose too!' She flung back the sheet and coverlet and sank her fingers into Terry's shoulders. 'I should have done the job properly up on the ridge. There was me thinking that Rosa was the only stumbling block—If I'd known, you would have gone over first, you bitch! Pushing Rosa would have been a damn sight easier then without you hanging on to her, with your snivelling pleas for her safety.' She yanked Terry up from the pillows. 'But don't think I'm going to walk away and leave you here sniggering at your good fortune.

You're going to pay for your sneaking ways——'

Jerked to her feet with such suddenness, Terry had nothing with which to combat the cruel awakening of all her body had suffered in the fall. She was giving in to the wave of nausea which engulfed her when a voice laced with a fury that outclassed anything that had gone before sliced into the room.

'That is *suficiente*, Verna.' The door, left ajar, opened and Rafael walked in. As Verna stood back and gaped he moved in swiftly and gathered Terry's crumbling frame close against him.

'But . . . but . . .' Verna mumbled, trying to smile. 'I heard you go . . . your car . . .'

'I sent the nurse off in it,' he explained with a thin smile. He lowered Terry back among the pillows, covered her and turned. 'I felt that there was a piece missing in—as you would say, the jigsaw—concerning the ridge accident. You have supplied it very neatly, Verna, with your more than abundant explanation, just now. I do not apologise for eavesdropping. When a matter of extreme seriousness has to be resolved there is sometimes no other way.' His jaw tightened. 'You are free to go, Verna. But I would advise you to leave the island at once and make yourself scarce in some other life. Otherwise I cannot promise that the facts that I have heard just now concerning Doña Rosa Perez . . .'

Verna had already backed away to the door. She hesitated for a moment, pulled herself up into a defiant gesture, then turned and hurried off.

After Rafael had watched her from the window, driving away in the hired car, he came to the bedside. 'Poor little Teresa *mia*.' He smoothed the hair from her temples. 'Sleep now and rest. And when you are well we will meet again.'

He went out of the room softly and closed the door behind him.

Terry lay with weakly thudding heart among the pillows. When Rafael had held her just now she had wanted to stay within the comfort of his arms, wrapped in his male nearness, for ever. Now at the thought the dampness filled her eyes. Verna had gone, and she was to stay, here under his roof. And she couldn't tell him that which she had kept hidden for so long.

She turned her face into the pillow and let the tears come.

Between long bouts of sleep Terry was aware of a gentle hubbub around the house. The nurse washed her and brought her meals that, even in her vague state, she sensed had been prepared in the villa kitchens by skilled hands. Occasionally a servant would smile about the room, quietly tidying and dusting.

With time Terry was able to sit up in the rose-pink velvet armchair and view the August days; the sun-drenched crags and foothills, shimmering mountains, and close at hand the semi-tropical foliage around the villa. She was spared the crushing heat out of doors by the cool flow of the air-conditioning which was regulated to changing conditions by a hand elsewhere.

When she was able to dress herself and walk a little the nurse left the villa and went back to her duties at the Alcudia clinic. It was then that Terry began to have feverish thoughts on her own departure. She had to get away before Rafael came to her, for she could never hope to stay immune to his dark searching glances now, she knew.

Her bags which she had packed and left ready at the cottage that fateful day had been brought here and all her things were hanging in the wall wardrobes. But it was useless to think about taking anything with her. All her strength would have to be conserved just to make a silent exit from the villa.

The colossal heat was another problem. She had been smitten by it on occasion when taking a stroll along the balcony outside her windows, and had returned indoors limp and thankful for the cool air of her room.

The evening would be the best time, she decided; dusk, when walking was bearable, though where she would go with no belongings wasn't really clear. All her quivering senses were tuned to just one thought. She had to get away before Rafael discovered that she wasn't, and never had been, an assistant at the villa. For one thing was sure, he would never forgive her if he knew.

The evening came when conditions were as favourable as they were ever likely to be. She was feeling considerably stronger if a little trembly and the villa was still and silent, with only the flashing birds enjoying the cool of dusk, and insects striking up their nocturnal chorus.

She had put on a dress of soft material chosen for its neutral colour of pale green to aid her escape across the gardens. For there could be no walking out of the front door. Her hair had bounced back into some kind of life, the deep waves framing her face as they had always done. If only she wasn't so pale!

With a last look at herself she decided there was no sense in decrying the fact that she might attract attention with her wan appearance on the road. She had to try somehow to put distance between herself and Al Azhar.

All was quiet in the house as she went downstairs. Everything was just as she remembered it, yet different somehow. That unexplainable atmosphere of warmth, the feeling of unseen hands, presences bringing to life what had once been mere furnished rooms, was everywhere. The villa had a heartbeat now, Terry smiled glistening-eyed to herself, one that she would never know the happy rhythm of.

She stepped out of the first available opening, a french window at the rear of the house where soft lawns would muffle her escape. The air was warm and heavy with the scent of blossom. Without pausing to worry about direction she stepped out and walked as quickly as her pounding pulses would allow.

There was a magnolia tree and other flowering shrubs a few yards away. She could rest a moment there and get her bearings. She had almost reached the spot when a figure appeared almost in her path out of an open doorway.

'Teresa *mia*! You are feeling strong enough to take an evening stroll?' Rafael's expression was one of hurt but humorous enquiry. He wore a monogrammed smoking jacket over open-necked shirt and slacks and looked relaxed. 'Come!' Because the words had seized up in her throat he led her gently across the lawn to the magnolia tree. 'It is here in these gardens where I planned to take my first kiss.' Before she could think of resisting he had become a warm, vibrating force. Before she had time to grasp at some defence he had enfolded her in his arms. 'Kiss me, Teresa. Kiss me as you did that night beside the *atalaya*.' His voice was softly compelling.

As weakness heightened the sentiment in her the feel of Rafael's nearness was a potently desirable thing. Never had she known the force of her love for him to reach such unmanageable proportions. The brush of his lips against hers was an agony of sweetness. She succumbed as she had never succumbed before, damning her chances of escape.

Held tenderly against Rafael, his arms enclosed her as she had always wanted them to hold her, as though for ever. Then he drew a little away and said happily,

'We will get married. No discussions are necessary.'

Terry felt the blood drain from her heart. She tugged out of his arms and stepped back. 'No, Rafael—I could never marry you.'

'Are you suggesting,' he said with a hard twinkle, 'that we should live in sin?'

'You don't understand,' she choked. 'I'm . . . not what you think I am——'

'I think you are adorable, sweet and *encantador*.' His twinkle deepened.

'I mean . . .' she blurted with a frantic look, 'I've deceived you—terribly.'

He drew her back into his arms, something in his expression moved by the look he saw on her face, and with a relenting gleam replacing the steely twinkle he said with a tender grin, 'Poor angel! I cannot let you go on suffering the delusion. I know that it was your sweet head that devised the interiors of our future home.'

'You *know*!' Terry stared, feeling a great weight sprout wings in her heart. 'But how?'

'I had guessed for some time that you were hiding something which caused you great distress.' His playful look fading, he rubbed his cheek against hers. 'But I didn't discover the cause until that day when Rosa Perez unknowingly endorsed my own feelings that what I had originally envisaged for the Villa Al Azhar had taken place. You see, I had said nothing to Verna about my seasonal theme for the interiors. It was only with her "assistant" that I had discussed my ideas of incorporating spring, summer and so forth in the decor of the rooms—And there they were, glowingly attracting Rosa's notice.'

Terry looked at him with a guilty blush on her cheeks. 'I just did it as I felt it should be,' she murmured.

'As *I* felt it should be.' His accusing gleam softened. After a moment he led her to a seat beneath the magnolia tree and said, 'Tell me about it, Teresa, this strange relationship which existed between you and Verna Wendell.'

As lightly as she could Terry related all that had taken place in the past year; her first encounter with Verna, their partnership, her own dislike of meeting people with a view to business, and Verna's suggestion that they work under different guises. When she had finished Rafael said with a lopsided smile, 'Foolish little *querida*, to want to hide a gift that most would willingly flaunt. And how I have had to suffer because of it! I knew you loved me that night beside the *atalaya*, but something held you back and I wanted to both shake you and kiss you with exasperation.'

He kissed her now with nothing like that mood, and when she could draw away she asked, half afraid to look at him with her star-bright eyes, 'Were you very angry when you discovered the truth about me and my work at the villa?'

'Like a raging Cordoba bull,' he laughed grimly. 'And yet the knowledge was not without a certain piquant *fascinación*. The girl I loved impressing her charming identity on the house where I would live. I did not know what to do. I decided to go ahead with the banking business and let the matter rest for a day or two. Then news of the ridge accident reached me.' His face darkened, his arms gripped her almost painfully. '*Cariña!* To come back and find you lying white and crumpled in a hospital bed! How could I be angry then? My only incensed concern was to find out who had done this thing to you. I was convinced there had been foul play, *mal intencion* on someone's part. The whole business reeked of it.'

'But Verna gave you a feasible explanation,' Terry said with a slight shiver.

'She did,' Rafael nodded, and held her close. 'But it lacked validity. Rosa never liked Verna. And Verna knew it. There was the key to the thing. I guessed that Rosa had discovered the truth about Verna's role as regards the villa. There too was a key. I was hoping that you would supply the answers when you opened your eyes. I should have known,' he smiled at her sternly, 'Teresa Heatherton always sticks by her acquaintances.'

His face darkened again, but this time with a kind of wounded humour. 'If you knew how consumed with jealousy I was over your constant concern for young Chandler! Everyone came in for your tender affection—even the holidaymakers. But the Marqués del Alcazar was always kept at a polite distance.'

'Poor Rafael,' Terry traced his lips with her finger. 'We'll have to make up for that neglect.'

'Is that a promise, *amor mia*?' His mouth travelled to the base of her throat, then he looked deep into her gaze. 'I knew that the girl who's eyes had filled with tears at the sight of a rotting wedding dress could not be indifferent to love. Do you remember that night in the Quiso mansion, Teresa? I loved you then.'

'I loved you too, Rafael,' Terry confessed shyly. 'But I had things on my mind. And there was Miriam. The whole town was alive with rumours of your forthcoming marriage with her.'

'The only person who really believed I would marry Miriam,' Rafael said, 'was Rosa Perez. Without her mother's domination Miriam will probably go off and marry someone of her own choice and live happily ever after.'

'And Verna?' Terry enquired steadily. 'You saw a lot of her.'

'Verna intrigued me,' he said with his hard smile. 'I could not relate her personality with all that was taking place at the villa. I was still trying to when I discovered that she had had nothing to do with the interior design. The fee that she would normally have been paid for the work will go into your bank account, of course. And with the—how do you say in your quaint tongue?—the perks from the job, I do not suppose Verna will be out of pocket.' He paused, then, impatient to get back to themselves, said, 'The townspeople will expect a grand wedding ceremony. Then I want to show you the whole of Spain. Over a lifetime, of course. It is here in Al Azhar where we will spend most of our wedded years. And that reminds me,' he stopped to fix her with a mock reproachful look. 'As an interior designer who has just completed her last work, do you realise you have made one serious omission in the house?'

'What is that?' Terry blinked.

'There is no nursery,' he glinted.

'But surely it is up to the *señor* to state his requirements,' she said demurely.

'We will attend to it. And if you wish you may have your last fling titivating the place.'

'I'll do that one thing,' she nodded, pink-cheeked. 'But nothing else. I want no more adventures in the world of interior design.'

'But will you not admit,' he drew her close, 'that this one has been worth it?'

'Mmmm!' she teased thoughtfully. 'I'll let you know in fifty years' time.'

'And every day of those fifty years,' he exacted from her menacingly.

Their kiss was long and lingering, after which, with a look at the darkening sky, Rafael said, 'We will go in and dress for dinner on our first night together in Al

Azhar. And tomorrow, if you are strong enough, we will go out for a drive, anything—even feed the fish on the hotel jetty if you wish,' he teased.

'There is one thing I would like to do,' Terry said, not needing to give it much thought. 'Could we go for a stroll in Lupin Valley?'

'But of course! How often have I walked with you there from a distance,' he admitted softly, 'when you have thought you were alone.'

With his arm about her waist Rafael led her indoors, and as she moved at his side Terry wondered if the girl of long ago, whose flowers filled the valley every spring, had been as happy with her love as she was now.

Harlequin® Plus
ALI BABA'S CAVE

Delgado's, where Terry goes to shop, is described as "an Ali Baba's cave," an apt metaphor when one considers the treasures Delgado's holds. The story of Ali Baba is part of *The Arabian Nights' Entertainments*, or *The Thousand and One Nights*, the ancient collection of tales told, so legend has it, by the beautiful Asian princess Scheherazade to her husband Schariar, a sultan, at bedtime. The story of Ali Baba is one of the more famous stories....

It seems that Ali Baba was cutting wood in the forest one day when he saw a band of thieves ride up to the side of a mountain. The leader shouted "Open sesame!" and a door in the rock opened to admit them. After the thieves left, Ali Baba went to the same spot and used the same magical words. The rock door swung open and revealed a cave; when he entered he discovered the thieves' treasure—gold, silver, jewels and silks. Although he was a poor man, Ali Baba took only three bags of gold. Then his brother, a wealthy merchant, discovered the secret and went to the cave with ten huge chests to fill. But his greed overpowered him, and he forgot the magical words to open the door and get out. The thieves returned and slew the unfortunate man. Discovering Ali Baba's identity, they went after him, as well.

With the help of a slave girl, Morgiana, Ali Baba was able to defeat the robbers, and have all the cave's treasures for himself.

Ali Baba had only to say the magic words, "Open sesame," to gain a fortune. Oh, were it only so easy for the rest of us!

Just what the woman on the go needs!

BOOK MATE

The perfect "mate" for all Harlequin paperbacks
Traveling • Vacationing • At Work • In Bed • Studying
• Cooking • Eating

Pages turn WITHOUT opening the strap.

Perfect size for all standard paperbacks, this wonderful invention makes reading a pure pleasure! Ingenious design holds paperback books OPEN and FLAT so even wind can't ruffle pages — leaves your hands free to do other things. Reinforced, wipe-clean vinyl-covered holder flexes to let you turn pages without undoing the strap...supports paperbacks so well, they have the strength of hardcovers!

SEE-THROUGH STRAP

Reinforced back stays flat.

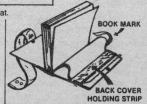

Built in bookmark.

BOOK MARK

BACK COVER HOLDING STRIP

10" x 7¼", opened.
Snaps closed for easy carrying, too.